'You'll feel d
have your own

'I'm not having ~~anything~~ she said simply enough, but did he detect a hint of defiance in her statement? 'My work's all I need.'

He'd forgotten about that. She'd mentioned it before. Was it really just because of her dedication to work? Or had her upbringing made her reluctant to have a family of her own? He found himself curious about it, but unwilling to question her on this topic now. They'd covered enough ground for one evening. 'Have lunch with me and Jules tomorrow. Get a taste of what life with siblings is all about.'

She laughed. 'Lunch would be lovely, but it won't change anything. Like I said before, you can't miss what you've never known.'

'The philosophical side to Jungle Tilly.'

'Is that really how you think of me? Jungle Tilly? You sound like my grandmother.'

He watched her for a moment, a smile touching the corners of his mouth. 'I think of you in a lot of ways.' His gaze trailed down to her mouth and lingered there. 'But most of all, I think of you as kissable.'

Emily Forbes is actually two sisters who share a passion for reading and a love of writing. Currently living three minutes apart in South Australia, with their husbands and young families, they saw writing for Medical Romance™ as the ideal opportunity to switch careers. They come from a medical family, and between them have degrees in physiotherapy, psychology, law and business. With this background they were drawn to the Medical Romance series, first as readers and now also as writers. Their shared interests include travel, cooking, photography and languages.

Recent titles by the same author:

EMERGENCY AT PELICAN BEACH
OUTBACK DOCTOR IN DANGER
CITY DOCTOR, OUTBACK NURSE
THE CONSULTANT'S TEMPTATION

A MOTHER IN THE MAKING

BY
EMILY FORBES

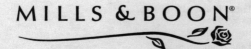

MILLS & BOON®

First published in Great Britain 2006
Harlequin Mills & Boon Limited,
Eton House, 18-24 Paradise Road, Richmond, Surrey TW9 1SR

© Emily Forbes 2006

ISBN-13: 978 0 263 84766 6
ISBN-10:   0 263 84766 7

Set in Times Roman 10 on 12 pt
03-1106-57790

Printed and bound in Spain
by Litografia Rosés, S.A., Barcelona

A MOTHER IN
THE MAKING

CHAPTER ONE

'YOU'VE been gone a long time.' The immigration officer wasn't making conversation. He was making an accusation.

He was taking his time with her passport, scrutinising each page before turning it with deliberate care to the next and scanning it as though it might be fake.

Tilly began to feel nervous, like she was trying to hide something. Her daypack was starting to chafe—she'd crammed more into her hand luggage than was proving wise. She swung it off her shoulder and tried not to look impatient as the guy with the official badge made sure she knew he was the *important* guy with the official badge.

'What's been keeping you away from Australia?'

OK, so he might think he was important but there was no way he was an intelligence officer. There were stamps by the zillions all through her passport, confirming her status as an aid worker—how else did he think she'd spent the last two years in Indonesia without having to leave and re-enter every three months to meet visa requirements?

'Work.'

He looked displeased at her reply and she decided she may as well play the game. Proving a point wasn't a great idea when he was the one with the little stamp-thingy she needed in order to pass through the imaginary gate next to his booth and grab her luggage.

'I'm a doctor. I work for foreign aid agencies. The entry visas are all in there.' She motioned to her passport. 'My last posting covered Central and Southern Sulawesi.' His face said he had no idea where she meant. 'In Indonesia,' she clarified.

He was watching her. Intently, like he was still assessing her story, like she really might have links to some sort of marginal group espousing violence.

'Now I'm home,' she added. He was still watching her like she might make a run for it. 'To work.' There, she'd said it, so it was real now, she was back. At least for a few months, long enough to ease her conscience about her gran.

She glanced around at the other tired travellers lined up at booths beside her. Were any of them being given as much grief? Maybe Immigration had always been like this and she'd become too used to the relaxed demeanour of the Indonesian villagers over the past two years. But it appeared as if she was the only one being held up. What was this guy's problem? She was an Australian citizen and a doctor, for goodness' sake. Didn't that count for anything?

She had a closer look at the other travellers. Most were dressed casually in deference to the burning summer sun that would greet them when they left the terminal, but none looked quite as dishevelled as her. She didn't have to touch her dark-blonde hair to know it was a tangled mess from the flight. Her face, too, was untouched by any trace of make-up. No one else looked quite as unkempt. Maybe that was it.

She rubbed her left temple distractedly, another headache was on its way. The guy flicked through the pages again and whacked his stamp down on the page like it had done him personal harm. If ever she'd seen a begrudging stamp smacked onto her passport, this was it. She grabbed the document before he changed his mind, and fled.

Her bag, a battered, dusty backpack that had seen better days, was one of the only ones left on the carousel by the time she'd made it through Immigration. She wasted no time in swinging it onto her back and heading towards Customs to join yet another queue. As the line inched forward, her ear tuned in to the broad Australian accent being used all around her. Despite her trepidation about living alone with her grandmother for the next three months without her granddad's mediating presence—the first time that had happened in the thirty years since they'd raised her from a baby—excitement started to swell through her. Not long now and she'd be on the bus to Noosa.

What was she going to find?

Tension.

That was the best answer Tilly had come up with since she'd asked herself that question a few days before.

Her morning walks along the beach fronting her grandmother Flo's property were a sanity-saving start to the day, she reflected as she picked her way through the ripples of waves lapping at the sand. She wasn't sure what she'd expected to find on her return. She'd known her grandfather's recent death wouldn't have softened Flo, but in the absence of her grandfather, Flo's no-nonsense ways and lack of warmth were difficult to manage. These walks were a welcome respite and she was hoping the fresh air and exercise would alleviate her frequent headaches. She was enjoying the small snatches of solitude, the only figure on the beach except for the two dogs running ahead. Slipping her sunglasses on as the sun rose above the horizon, its rays already strong enough to make their glare uncomfortable, she looked out to sea to find a man swimming there.

He was doing laps up and down from the cove to the rocks marking either end of this stretch of beach, a hundred metres or so out, slicing through the water with apparent ease while his dogs gambolled in the water or on the shore like the overgrown puppies she supposed they were. She'd seen him yesterday as she'd padded out of the trees onto the sand. He'd been jogging away from her through the shallows, his dogs either side of him. Barefoot, bare-chested and tall, with golden-brown skin, his well-toned arms pumping as he'd run. She'd stopped and stared without realising it. He'd finished his run and then crashed through the surf, which had been higher yesterday, until he'd been deep enough to dive under the waves. She'd watched him until he'd resurfaced a moment later and started his easy free-style to one end of the cove.

Which was where he was again today.

And there IT was, she thought as the increasing noise of buzzing engines brought her gaze around to the southern end of the beach. She waited for the two jet-skis to appear in their inlet, disturbing the otherwise tranquil morning.

She'd meant to ring the coastguard yesterday and lodge a complaint, but had forgotten once she'd got home. They'd appeared on the last two mornings, sending her pulse sky-high when they had first roared into view. True to form, as the machines came into view, the men—boys?—were being just as erratic in their driving and were in too close to shore. They were using the jet-skis to run at each other, the riders crouching, hunched over the handlebars, taking it in turns to head straight at the other one before swerving at the last moment, screaming and yelling their version of war cries. The noise of the engines, too, was vile. Too loud, too insistent, too out of place in the serenity of the cove.

Had they even seen the swimmer? Tilly searched for him and saw him stop and raise his head to look over to them for a moment, before putting his head down and moving again with his easy freestyle stroke, back to the opposite end of the cove from where they were messing about. If it had been her, she'd have got out of the water, but at least he was aware of the danger.

Calming her heart rate wasn't going to happen. Neither was sitting on the sand to think, so she picked up her pace—there might as well be some fitness benefit to the interrupted plans for her morning.

It must have lasted all of two minutes before the penetrating noise dragged her gaze back to sea, and so she saw it, one jet-skier heading at speed for the other. But this time there was no last-minute swerve and the machine was driven with a sickening crash into the side of the second jet-ski, catapulting its rider over the handlebars. She saw him land on his back, disappearing into the waves for a moment, before popping up motionless, face down in the sea.

The force hadn't knocked off the other rider but he was clutching at his ribs, yelling at his friend, who didn't respond, while the dogs sprinted up and down the sand, barking at the disturbance.

Tilly scanned the scene, tracking the riderless jet-ski, which was still running, circling the spot, creating a risk in swimming out to help. She ran down the sand to the water, wading in as she called out, 'Hey!'

Only the dogs responded, bounding over to her where they ran about in frantic circles, still barking. She waved her hand above her head, trying to get the jet-skier's attention. He'd have to come in and go for help. He was doing nothing out there for his friend and she had to get to him. 'Hey!' she screamed, louder, and this time he did look towards the shore. She saw him hesitate before he headed in, covering the hundred metres or so quickly, to the spot where she now stood knee-deep in the waves.

'Are you all right?' She resisted adding the 'you bloody idiot' that was on the tip of her tongue.

He nodded and she grabbed the handlebars.

'I'm a doctor. Let me go and check your friend,' she said as she motioned for him to get off the jet-ski. She'd ridden one a few times, it wasn't hard. She pointed at a path leading off the beach through the dense foliage edging the sand. 'Go as quickly as you can along that path. There's a house a couple of hundred metres or so up there. Someone's there, so ring for an ambulance, tell them there's been a jet-ski accident and your friend is unconscious.' The man nodded and ran up the sand and she turned the jet-ski without waiting to watch him. She'd deliberately not told him to alert the coastguard in case he did something stupid like run off, afraid of prosecution, but mentioning the jet-ski element should be enough for the ambulance officers to make the connection.

Semi-standing, feet flat on either side of the seat, she balanced on the running board and gunned the throttle. The machine moved with more force than she was expecting and she lost her balance momentarily, bracing her legs against the power of the jet-ski before managing to turn it to cut straight through the small breakers. Once she had the feel of the engine, the surf wasn't big enough to pose any difficulty, even with her limited experience, but she kept her eyes on the sea and her body tensed against any unexpected waves. To her right, she could see the swimmer cutting through the water with his decisive strokes, also heading for the accident scene. Relieved she wouldn't be facing a rescue on her own—she had no idea how she was going to heave a heavy, unconscious male out of the water onto the jet-ski—she slowed as she reached the young man, still floating face-down, the sea coloured slightly with his blood. At least they'd had the sense to wear life-jackets.

Checking that she wouldn't collide with the unmanned jet-ski still circling, its engine buzzing insistently, she reached the man's side and turned off her machine. She squatted, balancing across the seat, to grab the back of his life-jacket and attempted to turn him over. She wasn't getting off the jet-ski until the swimmer arrived, she wasn't taking the risk of losing her only anchor point out here. With her muscles braced, she just managed to roll him over until he was on his back. He was young, fifteen or so, she guessed, and the only source of blood she could see was from his nose—not facial or skull lacerations, as she'd feared. Hopefully, he just had a concussion and had also hit his nose hard, nothing worse. She had to get him out of the water so she could clear his airway and check for breathing and circulation.

Kneeling on one knee, the other bent, Tilly slipped her hands as best she could around the bulk of his life-jacket to grasp him under the armpits. Pulling with all her strength, she tried to heave him up onto the running board but only managed to nearly topple into the water herself against the deadweight of his body.

'Careful.' Tilly felt herself steadied by a strong hand and looked down into a face bathed in shadows, the sun still low in the sky behind him. The swimmer. 'Slide in and I'll get on and pull him up.' His voice was deep and broken by great breaths, his broad chest heaving as he inhaled, testament to his sprint to get there.

Tilly slid backwards off the craft, gasping as her body broke the cool water, then gasping again as the man put a hand out for a moment to steady her once more. It was just for a moment, and then he heaved himself onto the craft with an ease that belied his bulk. It had only been a moment but the touch had been electric. She could still feel the light imprint of his fingers on her bare skin, the thin straps of her bikini top offering nothing in the way of coverage as she swam around behind the injured boy. Holding onto the rocking craft with one hand, she supported him under his upper back with her other. As the swimmer grabbed him under the armpits and heaved, she trod water and gave what little help she could to hoist him out of the sea.

The man clearly didn't need her paltry assistance and had the boy lying on his side on the running-board of the jet-ski within seconds. Without hesitation, he lowered his cheek to the boy's face, listening for breath sounds before checking for a pulse, his large hands working deftly, his full mouth set in a determined line.

'Do you know mouth-to-mouth?' she queried. It seemed he knew what he was doing but she had to be sure. There was little she could do from the water and no room for her on the jet-ski, but if he didn't know CPR, they'd have to swap places. From where she was, she was sure now the rider wasn't just unconscious, he wasn't breathing.

'Yes.' Only one word but it was backed up by his actions. He was already slipping two fingers into the youth's mouth and clearing the airway, his actions measured and skilful. He knew what he was doing.

And he was successful. The rider vomited sea water and with a great shudder of the chest resumed breathing.

'Easy, mate,' he said as the jet-skier came to and started to struggle against his hold. 'You've been in a jet-ski accident, you're hurt. Stay still and we'll get you to shore.'

The boy groaned and relaxed, the struggle going out of him.

The swimmer turned to Tilly. 'We'll have to take him in on the jet-ski—can't chance waiting on the coastguard,' he said. 'I'll help you up.' He had one foot behind the seat, the other preventing the boy from rolling off the jet-ski, as he held a hand out to her.

'I'm not sure there's room for me.'

'We'll make room. It's a long swim, trust me on that.' He smiled at her and in that instant Tilly decided she'd fit on the jet-ski if it was the last thing she did. She took his hand and braced one foot against the machine as he pulled her from the sea as if she were weightless, catching her against the wet expanse of his broad chest, slick beneath her fingertips. She could smell sweat mixed in with the sea water, and another fragrance, sun-block, and then there was just too much gorgeous tanned skin right in her face for her to be able to formulate any thought at all.

Now there were three of them on a jet-ski built for one, all sodden, all slippery, and she wasn't at all sure how they could manage it. She was basically straddling his lap, face to face with him, as it was. Luckily, he had it all planned out.

'I'll hold our friend here and squat behind you. You'll have to balance as best you can and take us in—slowly, mind, so we don't all take a tumble. I won't have a spare hand to hold on.'

He eased himself back a little to give her room to turn and she moved until she was facing the handlebars, feeling her face burn as she straddled not only the seat but also him. She was half-standing, in nothing more than a bikini top and the shortest of shorts, both items dripping wet and the shorts clinging to her legs. Worse, the tops of her bare legs were level with his face. She knew, because as she started the craft and turned it carefully towards the shore, the movement rocked her back a little and she could feel the contours of his facial features on her skin.

This was no way to be close to a man she'd never met—or any man. It might only be a short distance to the shore, but the pained embarrassment was going to make her feel each metre as if it were a kilometre. She tried to concentrate on avoiding the other jet-ski, still droning around the accident site, and navigating their way through the low surf.

With every bump as the jet-ski crested each wave, the injured boy groaned, making her even more conscious of going as slowly as she could when all she wanted was to turn the throttle up full-bore and get to the beach as quickly as she could, especially once she saw the ambulance officers running out of the national park and down to the shore. It could only have been a couple of minutes, less maybe, but it seemed an eternity. When they reached the shallows and the swimmer stood to step off the jet-ski, his upper body moved along the length of her back as he squeezed behind her to lift the boy over the water and onto the waiting stretcher. Again, it was all over and done with in only a few seconds, but the mere thought of a man being in so many intimate positions with her in the last ten minutes was more stressful than anything else that had happened that day.

She stayed on the jet-ski, calming her breath and willing the redness in her face to abate. There was scarcely any part of her that the man hadn't seen or touched in some way or another, all necessary, all innocent.

The trouble was, it was her own body's reaction that had been anything but innocent. Instantly favourably disposed and craving more of the stranger's touch, that was the reality keeping her cheeks aflame. How that could be when she didn't think she'd

ever be able to look him in the face again, she didn't know.
Thank heavens there'd be no need to once she got off the beach.

'You OK?'

She jumped, startled to find the ambulance officers were
already crossing the beach with the young man on the stretcher,
leaving her alone with the swimmer, who was once again holding
out a hand to her, his dogs panting at his side.

She swallowed hard and took his hand, guilty at the rush of
sensation that the simple touch engendered, and let him lead him
off the jet-ski onto the shore. She couldn't touch him again
without introducing herself. 'I'm Tilly.'

'Good job out there, Tilly.' He let go of her hand when they
reached the sand, and motioned for his dogs to drop. 'Are you
sure you're OK now? Got your breath back?'

She nodded. 'I'm fine.' No self-respect left, she added silently,
that's all. 'And you?'

'That last sprint to the jet-ski almost did me in but I'll be all
right. Just a little older than I thought, not up for this surf-rescue
business any more.'

She laughed. 'Is that how you know resuscitation? You're a
lifesaver?'

'Not since I was in little Nippers.' He named the nation-wide
surf lifesaving club for children. 'And that was a few years back.
I'm a doctor. Actually,' he added, a grin spreading across his face,
'there aren't too many women named Tilly wandering about
these parts, so I'm guessing I'm not just a doctor, I'm also your
neighbour and your new boss.' He held out a hand. 'Jock Kelly.'

If her face had been pink before, it was emergency-services
red now as she slipped her hand into his outstretched one.

'OK,' she said, drawing the word out slowly while she put two
and two together and still came up with six. The touch of his grip,
firm but not overpowering, wasn't helping restore her equilibrium,
and she released the clasp after the briefest shake she could manage.

'You're Jock Kelly.'

'The very same.' He was shading his eyes with one hand as he looked down at her. Looking up, she could verify he was as tall and wide across the shoulders as she'd thought when she'd watched him yesterday. With an effort she focused on his shadowed face, when she really wanted to take a good look at him, now that the chaos and physical contortions of balancing on the jet-ski were over.

But the fact that so far he hadn't even allowed his eyes to wander from her face, admirable as that was, made it impossible for her to behave any differently, even if she was only curious. Faced with a relatively unclad female, not looking would be a Herculean feat for most men, but his gaze hadn't wavered and she relaxed.

She relaxed, the tension of the past half hour subsiding and she felt a bubble of laughter start in her stomach at the awkwardness of their meeting, and he saw the echo of the smile beginning on her lips and responded with a broad one of his own. Even in the shadows she could see it reached his eyes and warmed them. She was right—his smile was lovely and he was nothing less than delicious.

She waved a hand at the jet-ski in the shallows. 'This has been quite the job interview.'

'I think we cleared that step some months ago.' He dropped his hand from his face, his eyes crinkling against the glare of the sun, and all she could think was that when he was old and grey, even lines on his face wouldn't prevent him from being more-ish. 'We'll consider this morning your orientation day.'

She laughed up at him. 'Things have changed since I last worked in Australia. It's been a while since I had to ride to anyone's rescue on a jet-ski.' She paused. 'Not that I got to be the knight in shining armour once I got there.'

'Only because I'm brawn as much as brain, whereas I'd hazard a guess that you are weighted more…' he did flick a glance at her arms now, but there was nothing assessing about it, nothing that made her uncomfortable '…towards the brainy end of things.'

'Hey! I've single-handedly lugged my backpack through many a lonely mile and have the muscles to prove it.' Her teasing was mirrored in the upturned corners of his lips. 'They're just well hidden.'

He raised an eyebrow at her. He was laughing as he ran his gaze along her upper arms again. 'Clearly.' One of the dogs whined and stood to nudge at Jock's hand, and Jock bent a little to rub it behind one of its cocked ears.

'I'd best go and get these terrors a drink. You must need one, too. I'll see you at work tomorrow—you know where to go?'

She nodded. 'I spoke to Pam, the CNC…' Tilly waited for a confirming nod from Jock '…last week and she said to come into Outpatients and she'll get someone to show me around to start with.'

He gave a short nod. 'I'll catch you after the grand tour and take you through things in Outpatients. You'll be doing clinic there tomorrow afternoon.' He was looking beyond her into the distance now and frowning. It seemed as though his thoughts were elsewhere. The dog nudged his hand again and he shook his head slightly and looked at her again. 'Too much on at the moment, but that's not for you to worry about.'

'Hopefully I'll be able to ease the load.' She grimaced at her statement. She sounded like some sort of do-gooder and she detested hints of that mind set.

'That's why you're here.' He smiled at her but again, his mind seemed to have left the beach. He snapped his fingers. 'Batman, Robin,' he called, and his dogs leapt up, tongues lolling, tails wagging at a rapid pace as they looked up at him with adoration in their big brown eyes.

'Unusual names,' she said.

'Where one goes, the other follows, so it seemed an obvious choice. Mutts, both of them,' he said, but his tone and the way he was rubbing the larger dog behind his ear showed his fondness for them.

'I'd better head off,' he said as he straightened up. 'I'll see you tomorrow and let you know how our patient is. I'll go over soon and check.'

'You work Sundays?'

'Not officially.' His smile was wry. 'But there's usually something that'll get me in there on a day off. And today it's our young friend who rides a jet-ski with less skill than a toddler. But, then—'

'That's being offensive to toddlers,' Tilly completed his sentence for him and surprise touched his expression briefly before he tipped his head back in laughter.

'A co-worker on my wavelength. This…' he paused and rubbed at his jaw '…I can live with.'

The look he gave her was appreciative and she knew she'd enjoy working with Jock Kelly. If she could just forget about the first ten minutes of their meeting spent with her semi-naked and pretty much sitting on his lap as they'd bounced over waves together.

CHAPTER TWO

NO SUCH luck, she realised twenty-four hours later as her orientation tour came to an end. 'I barely recognised you with your clothes on.'

Jock. Speaking loud enough for anyone near Outpatients Reception—and there were plenty—to hear. Judging by the reactions, most of them had.

Embarrassing, yes, but despite the flush stealing across her face again, she couldn't help but laugh. Fortunate, or the gossip mill would really have started to churn if she'd seemed flustered or angry. 'I keep my rescue gear for special occasions.' Her tone was light, perfect for squelching rumours.

'You!' said Rebecca, who had taken Tilly on a whirlwind tour of the hospital, bar the outpatients department where they were now. 'You were the one who helped rescue that idiot on the jet-ski?' It was said with admiration, a change from her own response to Jock's statement.

'Craig,' said Jock, apparently admonishing Rebecca, who tried not to look sheepish until he continued. 'The idiot's name is Craig.'

Tilly laughed. Jock was shaping up to be great value. And not a bit less adorable in his work gear, covered in his white doctor's coat. After yesterday morning, she'd expected to feel even more exhausted than she'd been feeling over the last few months, but she felt better than she had in ages. The headache that had been plaguing her increasingly of late hadn't so much as tweaked at her temples and she was happy to chalk it up to Jock.

He handed a pile of folders to the receptionist. 'These are ready for filing. Can you pull out the folders for this afternoon in the next half-hour? I'll run through them with Tilly before clinic starts.'

He turned back to Tilly. 'Rebecca taking care of you?' He looked between them, his manner relaxed, friendly. 'Know your way around?'

'Admirably, to the first question,' answered Tilly, as she looked straight into his eyes that she saw now were dark grey, like the sea on a stormy morning. 'Heaven in a face' was the phrase that came to her. She stifled a laugh at the expression but it was an apt description in his case. He had eyes a girl could lose herself in. Her speech went onto autopilot. 'I'll let you know my answer to the second when I've had to get somewhere by myself.'

He smiled his response and said to Rebecca, 'Thanks for showing Tilly the ropes. I'll take it from here and I suggest you make a dash for the cafeteria before you head back to the ward. I have it on good authority Wanda has rustled up some of her raspberry slices today.' He looked at Tilly. 'Wanda is the resident patron saint of stomachs in the cafeteria.'

'Bye, Tilly.' Rebecca had taken a step to leave at the mention of the raspberry slices. It must be some slice to compete with Jock.

'Thanks for your help.'

'Bye, Dr Kelly.'

Jock waved at Rebecca and in the same instant placed his other hand on the small of Tilly's back and started walking, steering her with a gentle touch towards the offices from which she'd seen him emerge. 'I'll get the tour out of the way here then we'll have morning tea.'

'You don't want to go now? You might miss out on the raspberry slices, and from the way Rebecca almost ran for the cafeteria, I gather they are quite something.'

Jock smiled again, the sort of smile that said he had a satisfying secret.

'Let me guess. Wanda keeps you a special serving aside whenever she makes your favourites?'

He laughed. 'Shh, not so loud or we'll have an industrial relations dispute on our hands for favouritism.'

'What's my hush money?'

'Your own slice.'

'You're on. How was Craig the idiot yesterday?'

'He'll live,' Jock said with a smile that made her heart race. 'Broken ribs, broken nose, dislocated hip and mild concussion. Lucky for him we were there or it could've been a lot worse by the time his equally daft mate decided to act.' He touched her gently on the back and indicated they should get moving. 'Mad kids,' he added as he ushered her through an open door into what appeared to be his consulting room. 'Sixteen years old and think they're so omnipotent they can handle powerful watercraft at speed, doing stupid tricks.' He indicated the chair, opposite his own, which was behind his desk, where she should sit, which they both did. 'I remember saying exactly that about my brother, only with him it was water-skiing and speedboats.'

'You never went through the reckless testosterone thing?' She was intrigued.

'Nope.' He sent her a sideways glance and she couldn't tell if he was serious or not. 'I skipped straight from seven to seventy.'

'Then you're very well preserved for seventy,' Tilly quipped, and he laughed.

'Thanks. I work at it.' He pushed aside a mound of paperwork with a groan. 'It'll keep. Unfortunately,' he added, before turning his attention back to Tilly. Waving a hand to indicate the department, he said, 'None of this will be new.' He looked at her for confirmation and she nodded. Outpatient clinics were pretty much the same anywhere, at least in Western hospitals. 'Tour

OK? Signed all the thousands of documents needed before you can be allowed to sneeze here in Document Land?'

'Yes, to both. And I'm glad I'm not the only one overcome with document exhaustion. After Indonesia, the administrative protocol in an Australian hospital is a little overwhelming.'

'Not big on red tape over there?'

She shook her head. 'Lots for the aid agency I work with but once you're in the field, things are a little more…' she held her index finger and thumb together to make the point '…casual.'

'We don't want to scare you off on your first day so we'll ease you in this afternoon. You can get your bearings, one of the staff can run you through admin procedures and you can do some consults with me. I gather that other than vastly different facilities and the location, the actual work you've been doing wasn't too different than what you'll see here.'

She nodded. 'None of my placements have been in what the media like to call disaster zones. I'm not part of an emergency response team, the ones that respond to the aftermath of natural disasters or in war zones.'

'You're saying we won't be seeing you on the nine-o'clock news any time soon for heroic acts of saving lives?' He held open a door, gesturing for her to go first.

She walked into the consulting room as she answered him. 'The humdrum everyday business of saving lives isn't very newsworthy.'

'But no less worthwhile for that.'

'That's what I think. I've always been in smaller units in rural, very poor areas, where there might be basic self-sufficiency for food and water but the communities are too remote and poor to have much else, including medical care.'

'I'd like to hear more about your work,' he said. 'Maybe we can grab a drink after work some time?' He paused, watching her with a serious expression before his features lit up with another of his heart-warming smiles. 'Then again, you'd have a veritable fund of stories. Perhaps we'd better make that dinner.'

That was not what she'd been expecting when she'd come to work that day, which made it all the more lovely. Would it be too forward to suggest this evening? Probably, she decided, so she said instead, 'I'd like that. And I promise to weed out all the boring stories and only regale you with the ones worthy of someone brave enough to show interest.'

'It's a deal.' He tapped the pile of folders, indicating a return to work issues. 'But in the meantime, about your basic working week, on Wednesdays and Thursdays and alternate Fridays we'll be out on clinics, either you or me or both of us. Come to think of it...' he sat back in his chair, looking pleased with himself '...we're both going out to Cockatoo Gully on Wednesday, so let's aim for dinner then.'

She nodded. Excellent. Only two sleeps to wait.

'Good, it's a date.' She tried not to look too hopeful at his remark. It was just a throw-away line, something people said all the time, as evidenced by his immediate return to work matters. 'And then you're in the hospital Mondays and Tuesdays with every other Friday off.'

'Always in Outpatients?' She got her mind off the prospect of an evening with the gorgeous man in front of her and steeled herself to think only of work.

He nodded. 'After today you'll be on your own for most of the consults. We've got a backlog because Skye Radcliffe left earlier than expected, with pregnancy complications, so I'll do tomorrow and next week with you to catch up.'

'What would you normally be doing then?'

'You mean, where's the backlog going to build up while I help catch up here?' He was smiling, even though Tilly knew he'd spoken the truth.

Seemed like he handled stress all right, better than she did, Tilly couldn't help thinking. She knew the symptoms of tiredness and exhaustion she'd been suffering from were common in the field and was trying not to be too hard on herself for it—most people suffered knock-on effects from work at some stage. She closed her mind to those thoughts. After all, there had been no additional ill-effects from the drama yesterday, so maybe simply having a break from the field was all she needed.

Jock had turned to sort papers on his desk that he clearly hadn't been able to forget about and she wasn't sure if he'd forgotten to answer. He was muttering a little to himself and making a few notes. Something was on his mind and she didn't interrupt his thought process. Besides, it gave her the perfect opportunity to take a closer look at him, and he was everything she'd gone to sleep envisaging last night. Even the run of little lines furrowed between his eyebrows as he considered a stack of papers was appealing. Not to mention his tan, highlighted by his crisp white coat and dark eyes fringed by the long, dark lashes nature seemed always to reserve for men, not women.

Jock's natural attributes spoke for themselves whereas, according to her gran, Tilly's were in desperate need of some polishing. Flo could never accept that her granddaughter couldn't shake off all traces of living and working in remote regions of the world the moment she stepped onto Australian soil. The transition back to Australia was always a challenge, and making the mental shift to start thinking about how she looked took longer each time she came back.

Readjusting was an effort. So there was no way she'd ever be able to please her gran by whiling away a few hours at the local day spa. How could she justify spending an amount equivalent to an Indonesian villager's annual salary on such an indulgence? Giving priority to the superficialities of grooming was hard when she'd spent so long working in areas where the people had so little.

Which was why finding herself wishing she'd spent at least a *little* time attending to her appearance that morning was a shock. Then again, Jock had seen her at her worst yesterday, sopping wet, no make-up, unbrushed hair twisted into a messy ponytail, in her oldest running shorts and a threadbare bikini top.

Basically, he'd seen her in her 'fresh from the jungle' state, as her gran called it. At least she was decently dressed this morning—although without stockings, she was never going to please Flo on that point—and her hair was freshly washed and brushed. She touched her hair and felt a lock that had worked its way loose from the ponytail.

As she was tucking it back into the elastic band, Jock leant back and faced her, tapped his pen against his lower lip, oblivious to her wayward train of thought, and took up the conversation again.

'Admin stacks up. But, then, I'm always running on the spot where that's concerned.' He glanced back at his desk and shook his head to illustrate the point. 'My paeds consults get wildly juggled and Pam tears her hair out and then, of course, I've been trying to squeeze in the rural clinics that Skye used to do. The upshot is I have really long days.' He laughed. 'When I say it out loud, I can see why Pam's always on at me to get a life.'

Tilly laughed.

Jock made a bad attempt at looking doleful. The twinkle in his eyes gave him away. 'So she's been ranting about me already.'

'Afraid so. You must know that's an obligatory part of the tour?'

'To rant about me?'

'Let's not get too egocentric,' she teased. 'In any hospital tour, character summaries are as essential as the where, when and how stuff.' Which was true. Pam hadn't said anything more than that, but the young nurse, Rebecca, had let it slip that Tilly's new boss was the number-one target for single women at the hospital. But so far no one had had so much as a drink alone with him. And it wasn't for want of trying. What had she said? He appeared not to notice the most direct of overtures.

There was a knock at the door and Jock called out for the person to enter then said, 'Don't believe everything they tell you about me, unless, of course, you like what you hear.' He smiled at her as he spoke and Tilly felt a rush of pleasure at the attention.

The receptionist came in and handed Jock a pile of folders, keeping eye contact with him, her smile broad, and ignoring Tilly. From what she'd seen, and from what Rebecca had told her, Jock was not short on female attention within the hospital walls. 'These are for this afternoon's clinic.' Did she hold onto them a little too long as she passed them over? Tilly thought so, but Jock didn't seem to notice. He was probably used to it.

The young woman left and Jock started to leaf through the folders. 'We'll do most together, but the list is fuller than I thought, so, if you don't mind, I'll put a few aside and let you do them by yourself.' He looked up at her briefly. 'Is that all right?'

'No problem,' she said, and he went back to the folders, leaving her to her musings for the moment.

She was going to enjoy working here, even if she did find herself spending a minute or two in front of the mirror every morning. If her gran thought she was responsible for a slightly groomed granddaughter, she might even cease her nagging on the subject. More importantly, she thought as she looked across at Jock, she hadn't been so 'jungle-fied', another of her gran's favourite accusations, that she couldn't recognise the signs of an attraction like this.

There were reasonably regular dalliances in the field. Foreign aid workers were such a tight-knit bunch it would have been bizarre for attachments not to occur and the often trying circumstances made distraction almost a necessity. But an attraction that had her thinking about lip gloss? It had to have been in her adolescence she'd last felt like this and she'd forgotten just how delicious the feeling was.

At least, so far, he seemed like a good candidate for it. So far, he held up very well under scrutiny—a heart of gold and gorgeous to boot. He seemed almost too good to be true. Which meant he probably was. Everyone had at least one flaw. What would Dr Jock Kelly's be?

* * *

Day one had gone well. Too well, Tilly thought in retrospect, just as day two started to unravel.

She'd had an uneasy sense of having forgotten to do something but until she'd seen Pam, who the day before had been as nice as pie, bearing down on her in the lunch-room, she'd not been able to recall what.

'Dr Watson.'

Oops. Yesterday Pam had called her Tilly. 'Is something wrong?'

Exasperation wasn't a strong enough word to describe the look on the Clinical Nurse Consultant's face.

'The Daveys are waiting for you. I paged you fifteen minutes ago.'

Tilly was still drawing a blank but it was clear she'd missed an appointment of some sort. 'I'm sorry, but…'

From the expression on her face, Pam was thinking Tilly was more than slow-witted. Tilly was inclined to agree with her. '*Adam* Davey, fours year old. You sent him for a chest X-ray.'

'Ah. Yes.' The details were still vague, though. She'd clearly been more overwhelmed than she'd realised yesterday.

'He's back in Outpatients.' Pam stood aside in the doorway, obviously waiting for Tilly to get to her feet and get moving. Her frosty expression was enough to make Tilly hope she stayed on her good side in future and she half expected Pam to follow her along the corridor to ensure she didn't dawdle.

She waited until Pam was out of sight before retrieving her pager. There was a number on the screen and now that she saw it she remembered returning the page. But why she'd then sat down again was a mystery. There was no denying she'd forgotten all about the Daveys and she was at a loss to explain what had happened. She was obviously more tired than she'd thought.

Checking the pigeonholes in Outpatients, she found Adam's file and X-rays outside room four. Tilly knew the Daveys were no strangers to the hospital system. This was Adam's third visit in four months, and they would think nothing of being kept waiting. But she knew she hadn't been waylaid by an emergency and the fact that she had no good excuse weighed heavily on her conscience.

She scanned the X-ray report before pushing open the door. 'Sorry to keep you all waiting. I've got the X-ray results here.' Mr Davey had looked up as she entered but Mrs Davey kept her gaze down.

Tilly slid the films out of their envelope, selecting one and slipping it onto the light box. 'This is a photograph of your lungs, Adam.' Adam was lying listlessly on the bed but looked over as she pointed to the X-rays. 'See these two balloon shapes?' Tilly traced the outline for them to see. 'Your lungs are supposed to be full of air, that's what makes them look black in the picture. Can you see these white spots in here?' Tilly pointed at several coin-shaped spots. 'That's fluid, like water, sitting in your lungs and making it hard for the air to get in and out. That's what's making it hard for you to breathe.' Tilly directed her gaze at Adam's parents. 'I see in the notes that this is Adam's third chest infection in as many months. I actually think it's been more like one long infection and he's now suffering from pneumonia. We can treat it but I need to admit him to hospital.'

Mr Davey looked anything but impressed with that news and he grunted. 'Hospital.' She wasn't sure whether it was a dismissal of her advice or a question, so she assumed it was the latter.

'Adam needs to be in hospital for us to give him the antibiotics he needs.'

'Dr Radcliffe and Dr Kelly give us antibiotics for him at home.' Adam's dad didn't say it, but she could hear the question in his words, *So why are you telling us something else?* They didn't trust her. If they knew she'd all but forgotten about them, they'd have even more reason to question her.

'The antibiotics Adam's been taking haven't fixed the problem. He needs a stronger course of treatment and we need to give them through a drip.' She kept her voice at what she hoped was a soothing, confidence-inspiring level. 'And I need to run some more tests.'

Adam's dad looked the very picture of suspicion at that announcement. His wife was yet to make eye contact with her but Tilly could see tears glistening as she held the young boy's hand.

She went on, hoping she'd be able to explain herself. 'I'm worried about infection in Adam's lungs. We need Adam to cough up some of the fluid so we can send it to the lab for tests. The white spots of fluid you can see can easily become infected—basically little pockets full of pus. If they're infected, it can lead to scarring in the lungs, which causes permanent damage. The tests are non-invasive but we need to get some samples.'

'We live out at Cockatoo Gully, that's two and a half hours away.'

She bit her lip. She knew she couldn't be too authoritarian with the Daveys. Mr Davey had been pretty good at pressing her for answers but they needed to feel they were making the decisions, not having her impose her will on them. 'Adam has had too many infections and it's clear he's really battling despite the care you've taken of him and the treatment he's had so far.' She paused for a moment, not wanting to rush them. 'I want to minimise the risk of permanent damage and the best way and the safest place for Adam now is here. I know that's hard, especially with you living so far away. If you like, I'll speak to Dr Kelly before you decide.'

Mr Davey gave a grudging nod of thanks in response to her offer and Tilly went in search of Jock. She didn't have to search far—he was walking towards her down the corridor.

'I was just coming to see how you're faring. Any troubles?' His tone was smooth but his eyes were cool, assessing. Had Pam said something? Tilly decided she couldn't worry about that now.

'No-o.' She hesitated. 'But I was coming to get a second

opinion from you for the Daveys.' She filled him in on the latest developments with Adam.

'I'll come take a look.'

'Thanks.'

Jock held the door for her before following her into the treatment room and greeting the family, who looked relieved to see him. Even Mrs Davey glanced up in greeting and the atmosphere in the room seemed to relax a little.

Jock examined the X-rays and agreed with Tilly's recommendations without hesitation, whereupon Mr Davey capitulated at once. 'And that's the difference trust makes,' Tilly muttered to herself. She'd have to get used to it. Trust wasn't something that could be forced or rushed. If she gained the trust of even a couple of people within the aboriginal communities she'd be working with, word would spread that she was OK.

'Why don't we take you to Admissions and get Adam sorted out?'

Mr Davey stood up and it was clear he'd be taking charge while Mrs Davey stayed with their son. 'The girls at the front can check with the caravan park for some accommodation for you, too. Tilly will come back and see Adam the moment he's in the ward.' Jock patted Adam on the shoulder and gave Tilly a glance. She knew then that Pam had said something but she had no excuse and certainly wasn't about to discuss her tardiness in front of her patient, so she kept quiet.

Jock walked Mr Davey to Admissions and left him there after a brief discussion.

Tilly hung back, not sure of her role now, whether she should get back to the clinic. She was sure she had time for a break, but then, she'd been sure she'd had five minutes to spare when she should actually have been with Adam. Jock broke into her reverie. 'There's something I'd like you to see.'

He wasn't smiling, but neither was his expression unkind. She breathed a sigh of relief. She wasn't going to get bawled out or be given the cold shoulder on her second day.

'I'd better check back with—'

He interrupted. 'You've got ten minutes to spare.'

He gestured for her to walk beside him and they headed out of the clinic area. 'Your choice of treatment was spot on. The hardest thing around here is often getting the parents to separate from a sick child. At the moment there isn't an alternative, but I want to show you an option we'll have in the not-too-distant future.'

Silence fell between them and she felt compelled to fill it. She touched his arm as they walked and said, 'I'm sorry I was late.' She didn't want to add an excuse—what could she say? She'd forgotten?

'I know it can take a while to find your feet in a new place. And I know it's been a while since you've worked in a setting like this.'

They could both hear the words 'but don't let it happen again' hanging in the air between them and Tilly's impression of him rose a few notches higher when it became clear he wasn't going to say them out loud. He couldn't be perfect, she was sure of that, but so far he seemed pretty close. He seemed happy to let the topic slide, so she did, too, turning her attention to where he was taking her.

They were walking out of the outpatients building now, along the external passageway, to the main building. The hospital had started life as several individual, single-storey buildings that had, at some stage, been connected by a series of covered walkways, no doubt to protect people from tropical downpours and the harsh Australian sun. Outpatients and the allied health department were on one side of the main building with the emergency department on the other.

'How was your morning overall?' he asked as he led her through the main building past Administration and the general medical and surgical wards towards Paediatrics and Maternity.

'Pretty good. There was only one terror child. Not his fault really, he needed some boundaries set,' she replied.

'I've learnt to give them the benefit of the doubt. I think I'm scared it might be my children one day being described as the terrors.'

'I don't have to worry about that.'

'How can you be so confident? They might be right little horrors,' he teased.

'Easy. I'm not going to have children.'

Tilly waited to see whether her revelation would be answered with a stunned expression or an attempt to persuade her otherwise. Invariably, people had one of the two responses.

'Is that right?'

She nodded.

'Why not?'

There. He was going to find out her reasons and try to convince her to change her mind. It was amazing how many people assumed they knew best, assumed they knew what she should do with her own life. She gave her standard reply, not necessarily the whole truth, but it was usually enough to satisfy people.

'I don't think I could be both a mother and a doctor to the best of my ability and since I don't ever plan on giving up work, I've made my choice. Although that terror child this morning was almost enough to put me off children altogether.'

'Fair enough.'

She did a double-take at his words. That was it? No argument? No telling her she'd change her mind when she met the right man? That was the most popular of the standard responses. But she'd never had a 'Fair enough' before. She slowed down—they'd reached the paediatric ward, which she assumed was their destination—and waited for him to quiz her further but he continued walking. Without comment he headed through the department towards a door marked 'Emergency Exit' at the end of a passage. He stopped there and entered a code to deactivate an alarm, before holding the door open for her.

'After you.'

Tilly passed through the doorway, surprised to find herself still indoors. They were in a large, newly built but not yet completed room. The floors were bare concrete and electric cables were hanging from the walls, obviously waiting for power sockets to be fitted. Ahead of her Tilly could see two doorways leading to other rooms.

'Where are we?'

'This is the Noosa District Hospital's family unit. Or it will be once it's finished. Come and see.'

Excitement and pride were evident in his voice, his enthusiasm even seeming to permeate his energy and put an extra spring in his stride. Thoughts about her decision to remain childless were clearly not bothering him and she wasn't sure what to make of that. Was he more discreet and less pushy than most people? Or just not interested?

Then she looked around her properly and her thoughts shifted, too. The area was exciting—large, open and full of light. It was as yet unfinished, but there was an energy about the space that grabbed her imagination. 'This was your idea?'

'My dream. I've seen these types of facilities in larger hospitals and I'm convinced it helps speed up recovery for children to have their families nearby. We see a lot of children, like Adam, from outlying areas for whom hospitalisation means separation from their families. They need another option. It's been a long-held dream of mine to give it to them.'

'What will the set-up be?' She was intrigued now by the unit and even more so by the man in front of her. People with a vision always entranced her. Jock, it seemed, was brimful of vision. And drive.

'The unit will be able to accommodate two families. This will be the communal lounge and we'll have a kitchenette over there.'

Jock gestured to the far side of the room. 'Meals are often a stumbling block—the kids want food they're familiar with and there's no way the hospital kitchen can cook individual meals for everyone. This way the families have an opportunity to cook basic meals, which is all kids want, and encourage them to eat.

'The bedrooms are through here.' Jock led the way. There were no lights as yet but the rooms were flooded with natural light. The windows looked out onto the hospital gardens, planted with native trees and shrubs that would attract plenty of birdlife.

'It's a gorgeous outlook. Very peaceful.'

'Good for the spirit,' he added, his voice full of life and cheer. 'Each bedroom will have one hospital bed and a bed for a parent as well. There'll be call bells for the nursing staff, just like in the wards, but the parents spend so much time in the paeds ward that this will help to make them more comfortable.'

'When will it be completed?'

'As soon as we've raised enough funds to pay for the final fit-out. Government funding has been promised to cover the cost of hospital equipment but things like the kitchen, lounge suite and soft furnishings have to come from fundraising.'

'Whose job is that?'

Jock spread his arms out. 'Yours truly.'

'So, as well as heading the paediatric department and travelling around the countryside, you're the king of fundraising?'

'The king of fundraising,' he repeated. 'I like the sound of it. Think I can get the staff calling me that instead of "Doctor"?'

She shook her head, laughing. 'No chance.' She didn't add that the staff she'd met so far would probably agree to do it, so devoted were they to him from what she'd seen.

'Worth a try.' He went on, his mind already back on the unit. 'This is my baby. I can't ask people to volunteer time or money if I'm not prepared to do the same. As it stands, there's nothing I won't do, nothing legal, anyway, to get it up and running.' He walked on through, pausing in the bedrooms to look out the windows, and Tilly guessed he was trying to picture how it would all look when it was completed. 'This is where I would like to have been able to put Adam.'

He led her back to the main area. 'So there you have it. This facility should enable us to work with the families of chronically ill patients and make separation unnecessary. Seriously ill children would still tend to end up in Brisbane but having this facility may allow us to keep some closer to home.'

'I'm impressed.' And she was. He'd left her filled with new excitement about working there, working with someone who could think outside the box and make dreams a reality. 'It's a fabulous set-up.'

'Thanks. I wanted you to see where the hospital is heading. I think it's a step in the right direction.' He glanced at his watch, a plain silver model, sleek on his broad wrist. 'You'd better check on Adam.'

'Of course.'

He smiled a goodbye and turned on his heel to leave, walking only a few paces before coming back to her. 'Don't forget we've got the overnight trip to Cockatoo Gully tomorrow.' She hadn't forgotten but after the incident with the Daveys it seemed he felt the need to double-check on her. 'I was planning on collecting you at 7.30 a.m. It's a fair drive.' He smiled. 'But, then, you already know that.'

She nodded. 'Although it's been a long time since I was out that way. It'll be good to see it again, see some old friends.'

'They're looking forward to seeing you, too. I told Eunice last time I was there you'd be helping out. I know she's Flo's oldest friend but I hadn't done the maths to work out she'd helped your gran bring you up.' He made a bad attempt at looking disappointed. 'Of course, she already knew you were coming back. Flo had already beaten me to it with the news.'

'As if a man could beat the power of two old female friends keeping up with each other's lives.' She laughed at the hammed-up, defeated expression on his face. 'You never stood a chance.'

'Can't give me a scoop on something?' His expression was mock-hopeful.

'No chance. Nothing to tell.' They were grinning at each other, the awkwardness of earlier forgotten, and now they were back to the easy camaraderie they'd slipped into almost from the moment they'd first met, or at least once she had recovered her self-esteem after the semi-naked jet-ski ride. Jock was just like that. 'But if something juicy happens, you'll be the first to know.' And she meant that, most sincerely, because she was just starting to realise how much she was hoping the something juicy would directly involve him.

CHAPTER THREE

TILLY saw the dust rising through the trees, indicating Jock's imminent arrival, and the anticipation that had been flickering away inside her doubled. She was packed, ready for the trip to Cockatoo Gully. She watched as he pulled his Land Cruiser to a stop beside the house, watched him swing himself out of the driver's seat. He was dressed in denim jeans, stockman's boots and a short-sleeved shirt. He looked more like a jackeroo than a doctor but, then, most of the men around here dressed like that. In fact, not just the men. Her outfit wasn't dissimilar. Jeans, T-shirt and a polar-fleece vest to ward off the morning chill. It was almost a uniform. A uniform for country folk.

Not many of them wore it as well as Jock, though. Tilly was treated to a very pleasant rear view as he reached into the four-wheel-drive. He turned, Akubra hat in hand, the final piece of the uniform.

He jammed it onto his head.

'Morning.' He smiled when he saw Tilly on the veranda, the brim of his hat obscuring the upper part of his face, leaving his eyes in shade. He looked intriguing. A man's man. Boy, but she loved her job. 'Ready to go?'

'Is that all you need?' he asked, picking up Tilly's small over-night case and medical bag. For a moment Tilly wondered whether she *had* packed everything. She'd made a list and checked each item off twice. She definitely remembered doing that. She was writing more lists these days. She used to pride herself on her excellent memory, but now she feared list-making was fast becoming a habit. No, after the incident with the Daveys, when she'd missed their appointment at the hospital, it looked like it might be a necessity. The list was in the pocket of her jeans. She was tempted to take it out and check it one more time, but she resisted the impulse. She'd checked and double-checked. She was ready.

'I'd better say goodbye to Gran.' Tilly heard the screen door bang behind her as Flo came onto the veranda. She turned and saw Flo holding out a gift-wrapped parcel and walked back to take it.

'Don't forget to take Eunice's present,' said Flo, waving to Jock as he called out his greetings. Of course they knew each other, thought Tilly. They were next-door neighbours even if their properties were much further apart than in the suburbs.

'I was just coming back for that,' Tilly fibbed. She'd completely forgotten about the gift for Flo's old housekeeper. Eunice had run Tilly's childhood home with military precision but she'd been much more than a housekeeper. She'd been a second mother to the orphaned toddler and Tilly knew Eunice loved her almost as much as Flo did.

Then again, she was going on a work trip and it was reasonable that her mind was focused on that. There was no need to make a big deal over forgetting to pack a gift, she told herself. There was no need to let the incident with the Daveys make her blow everything out of proportion.

It was fine. She was fine. She'd been fatigued from aid work and now she was getting used to both a new job and to readjusting back to life here. All of that was tiring, mentally and physically. Another week and she'd be on top of those things again. Then there'd also been her grandfather's recent death. She'd said her goodbyes in the month she'd returned to spend with him last year when he'd been diagnosed with terminal cancer, but the feeling of loss was still there. Was it any wonder she was coping less well than usual?

She pecked her grandmother on the cheek—when she'd tried in the past to get beyond Flo's barriers and embrace her, it had always felt embarrassingly awkward so she didn't try any more—before picking up her straw hat. She'd grown up on the cattle station with an Akubra hat almost permanently on her head, but after seven years at university in the city and six years overseas she no longer felt like a local. 'Bye, Gran. See you tomorrow.'

'Give Eunice my love,' said Flo as Tilly walked to the four-wheel-drive.

She couldn't help the twinge of hurt her grandmother's words had generated. Why did Flo's old friend merit her love and not her granddaughter? She'd never signed one of her letters to Tilly 'With love', only ever 'From your grandmother'. She brushed the thought away as unimportant. Her grandmother wouldn't change and she'd always taken care of the external aspects of Tilly's life, ever since her parents had died when she'd been a baby. Flo couldn't be faulted on that, but sometimes Tilly couldn't help wishing her grandmother actually *liked* her, too.

Jock opened the back of his vehicle and tossed her bags in. The boot was jam-packed. Tilly could see swags, boxes, insulated cartons, water bottles and tool kits. A couple of spare tyres were chained onto the roof rack. 'Did you want to drive?'

'No, thanks, I'm happy to be a passenger.' She could feel the beginnings of a headache but resisted the urge to rub her left temple. Roll on, adjustment period, she thought, anxious to feel like everything was on an even keel and she'd be back to feeling like her old self, brimful of health and energy. She put her sunglasses on, grateful that they'd be driving west, away from the morning sun, and climbed into the passenger seat. After seeing the amount of gear in the boot, she was surprised to find that she had a clear space around her in the car. Obviously Jock had a system and everything had a place.

Jock closed her door and took his seat behind the wheel. He started the car, driving off with a beep of the horn and a wave for Flo.

'You've done something to your hair. It looks nice.'

Tilly laughed. 'I brushed it.'

He looked startled. 'That's it?'

'Actually, no. Gran gave it a trim, too. My luscious locks hadn't seen scissors in a while and Gran was having sleepless nights about it, so I did the granddaughterly thing and let her attack me.'

He gave her a look that might have been full of appreciation. Or it might not. He turned his attention back to the road before she could read him, but after a moment he gave her another once-over and when she met his gaze, she could see more than simple interest in what her hair looked like.

She knew it was just a boring, no-frills haircut but she liked the feeling that he'd noticed. And noticed her.

'It really does suit you. I had no idea a hairbrush could make such a difference,' he teased, and she wondered whether it was to take away the awareness of each other that had seemed to fill the car when their eyes had met.

'Thanks. But now I'm feeling like I must have looked like the mess Gran said I did beforehand.'

He laughed. 'I'll ease up on the hair comments. I get the feeling you're not one to fish for compliments.' He paused and sent another glance her way. 'Not that you'd need to do much fishing.'

'Oh,' was all she could think of to say. Was he saying she was good-looking? She'd had her share of admirers but she'd always assumed it had been because options were limited in the field.

It was time to change the topic before she started musing about whether her colouring made her a winter or summer person. 'So what's on our agenda today?'

The smile around his lips said he knew she'd felt uncomfortable with his compliment but he said nothing more on that subject. 'General clinics. It's fairly informal. The community knows we'll be there today and there will be people waiting when we arrive. We don't bother with appointments, it's on a first come, first served basis. You'll find it's a social occasion as much as anything for many of them. They're happy to sit and wait while they catch up on gossip.'

Tilly picked at some imaginary lint on her jeans. She knew Jock would be expecting a response from her but she was suddenly apprehensive about returning 'home'.

'You're not nervous about the clinic, are you? You'll know most of the people.'

'But they knew me as Tilly from Dalgerie Station, not Dr Watson. It's a completely new situation.'

'You'll be fine. You grew up with these people.'

'Not exactly. One hundred kilometres down the road. And it's what's changed since that bothers me.'

'You'll find nothing much has changed. Everyone will remember you. Kylie, Eunice's granddaughter, will be on the front desk. She'll find the patient records for you and tell you whose turn it is. I imagine the system, if one can call it that, isn't dissimilar to how you worked in Indonesia.'

'Probably not, although, like I said, mostly we didn't even have any paperwork.'

'My idea of perfect working conditions.'

'Ye-es.' She drew the word out. 'In some ways, but it actually took a bit of getting used to. You don't realise how much you rely on being able to double-check things like patient histories. Patients are hopeless at remembering their own symptoms. Have they had this same rash before? Do they have any allergies? Was it this child or another one who had conjunctivitis?'

'So every patient is like new?'

'Pretty much.' She'd become accustomed to the working conditions in the field but talking about it now, she wasn't surprised she had some memory lapses. No one could be expected to remember everything about patients without some sort of record to jog the memory. She felt her anxiety about forgetting about the Daveys and Eunice's present settle even more. She was only human and if she concentrated hard until she felt on top of the new job, it wouldn't happen again.

'Today should be a breeze, then.'

'Absolutely,' she said, and the confidence in her tone was real. She felt good about the day ahead and her ability to do the job. All she needed to keep her tiredness in check was to keep focused.

Maybe it would have been wise to have had more of a holiday before jumping straight into this position, but they'd needed her. And while financially she had enough to manage without working for a few months, especially when she had a roof over her head with her gran, she'd never been one to do nothing. Sitting still wasn't her style and Flo also had never encouraged idleness. Besides, sitting next to her was one very good reason to go to work each day. Jock Kelly.

They lapsed into a comfortable silence. Tilly's headache was still bothering her and she was happy to sit quietly and try to distract herself by mentally listing the things she liked about Jock. He was observant, a good listener, smart, with a sense of humour, a fair boss, considerate, compassionate and *gorgeous*. Flawless, so far. Maybe he wasn't house-trained. She hadn't been inside his house—maybe it was a complete mess. Although if his car was any indication, his house would be just as organised. Still too good to be true.

'There are some painkillers in the glove box, if you need a couple.' Jock's voice broke the silence.

'What?'

'Painkillers. For your headache.'

'What makes you think I've got one?'

'You've been very quiet and you keep rubbing your eye.'

Observant and considerate.

Tilly found the packet and popped two capsules from their foil, swallowing them with a gulp of water.

'Close your eyes. I'll wake you when we get there.'

'You don't mind?'

'My motives are purely selfish. I want you recovered by the time we start work.' He winked as he spoke but Tilly resolved to cover up any malaise in future just in case he was serious.

True to his word, Jock woke her up as they crossed the bridge leading into town. At first glance nothing much had changed, the same dusty streets lined with the same tired, weatherboard houses, some with gardens, but most without. But as they approached the centre of town the dirt road suddenly turned black.

'I don't believe it! The road's been tarred.'

Jock laughed. 'Don't get too excited. It only lasts about two hundred metres, but there have been some other improvements.'

Tilly's jaw dropped as she saw several new buildings on both sides of the road. 'Wow.'

'New council offices, with a decent library and dedicated community health rooms, upgraded school buildings and the pick of the bunch, as far as the local kids are concerned, is the new indoor sports centre.'

'This is amazing. Who paid for it all?'

'The local council has worked really hard getting government grants—they're half way through their ten-year plan.'

'What's next?'

'They've started work on an aquatic centre. We can go for a walk after the clinics and I'll show it to you.'

'I'd like that.'

Jock turned into the council car park. 'Let's get sorted. With two of us working, we should be able to sneak away a bit early, but the sooner we start the more time you'll have to look around. Good, here's Kylie.'

Tilly saw an attractive, dark-skinned girl walking towards

them, but it took her a moment to realise that it was Kylie—she couldn't believe her childhood playmate, Dean, could have an adult daughter.

'My goodness, you're all grown up!'

'Hello, Tilly.' Kylie laughed while she hugged her. 'You haven't seen me for six years. Kids do tend to grow up.'

'You're making me feel old! How are you? How's your dad?'

'He's good. Still working out at the mine. Gran's coming past later to see you.'

They followed Jock inside while trying to catch up on six years of news. Kylie showed Tilly to her treatment room and re-appeared with a cup of tea.

'Why don't you drink this before I send your first patient in? It's herbal, for your headache.'

'How did you know?'

'Dr Jock told me.'

'For a minute there I thought you might have inherited your gran's sixth sense.'

'Nothing like that, though sometimes I wish I had.'

Tilly drank her tea and a steady stream of people started coming through the door. Mostly they had coughs and colds, gastro bugs or needed antenatal checks. Nothing too challenging but Tilly was pleased to take a break for lunch when she heard Eunice arrive. Eunice, one of the few constant influences in Tilly's life, even though their times together were now few and far between. But it hadn't always been so.

'Eunice!' Tilly, filled with the warmth of being reunited with someone special to her, was wrapped in a reassuring hug within moments of the older woman entering the room.

Eunice released her only to say goodbye to Jock, who was excusing himself on the pretext of letting them catch up. Tilly took care to just give Jock a causal wave and not to watch him leave. Eunice needed no clues to sense her attraction and Tilly wasn't ready for Flo to start getting excited about something that wouldn't happen. There was no reason to think that her attraction to Jock was anything other than one-sided.

'How are you? You haven't changed a bit.' And she hadn't. The years always seemed to tread lightly for Eunice.

'I'm good. A bit arthritic these days but I can't complain. But you look tired. And pale. Working too hard? Not eating properly?'

Tilly shrugged the questions off with a laugh. She didn't need Eunice's sharp eyes trained on her health, either. 'I'm fine, just readjusting to life back here.'

'Are you back from the jungle for good?'

Tilly grinned at Eunice's description of her work environment.

Eunice wagged a finger at her and Tilly knew she was about to answer her own question. 'Ah, still not sure.'

'Why do you say that?'

'I can feel it.' Eunice was nodding her head. 'You still aren't sure what you want. You're finding your way.'

Tilly smiled. She knew Eunice had plenty of intuition, and although she didn't believe in a sixth sense as such, she'd often been on the receiving end of Eunice's 'feelings' and found them to be spot on. Somehow, Eunice was always able to read her.

'I haven't decided what to do,' Tilly admitted. 'I'm on a three-month contract so I'll see how Gran and I are getting along at the end of that. I might stay or I might go back overseas. I didn't want Gran to be on her own at this time but you know we haven't always been close.'

'You haven't resigned from the agency? '

Tilly shook her head. 'I didn't want to do that, not yet. They were happy for me to take a break. This way I can easily return without having to go through all the red tape again.'

'You need to do what you feel will make you happiest. You never know, you might find what you're looking for right here.' Eunice glanced out the window; they could see Jock walking along the street. For all that Eunice's glance had looked coincidental, Tilly knew it wasn't. She averted her gaze, not wanting to confirm the old lady's suspicions, but knowing, too, that Eunice needed no confirmation. She'd already be confident in her feeling about Tilly. 'Work isn't everything.'

'It's always been enough for me,' Tilly replied.

'There'll come a time when you'll start to wonder if you should be doing something for yourself.' Eunice was still looking out the window, following Jock's path. 'Does he know you're not well?'

'Pardon?' Tilly knew she'd just confirmed Eunice's suspicions with her startled reaction.

'I can tell. You're not well. Does Jock know?'

'I'm fine, Eunice, really. I just had a bit of a headache.'

'There's more to it than that and don't go denying it. If you haven't said anything to Dr Jock, what about your grandmother?'

'I'm not about to burden her with anything more and, besides, it's nothing. I have to make an appointment in Brisbane for a medical check—it's routine on return from foreign aid work—and they'll give me a thorough going over.'

'You need to be honest with them about your health and make sure they check your head.' Eunice was standing beside Tilly now and placed her hand on the left side of Tilly's head. 'There's something here.'

Eunice's hand was covering Tilly's temple and ear, the site of her headache, and the fact that Eunice had so accurately pinpointed it worried Tilly more than any of her symptoms had to date. She'd satisfied herself that her symptoms—the headaches, the forgetfulness, the tiredness—were just due to fatigue and the stress of her grandfather's death.

She was still sure things would settle down once she got some rest, despite the fact that her tiredness hadn't improved, she'd forgotten a couple of things now and her headaches seemed to be becoming more frequent. Eunice was right. She had to get it checked out, but she knew the diagnosis would be simple: she had overdone it and needed to get some rest.

'What would you tell your patients to do?'

Tilly could see Jock returning to the clinic and she did not want to have this discussion in front of him. 'I promise, I'll go to Brisbane and get properly checked, but can we forget about it until then?'

Eunice thought about it for a moment, looking into Tilly's eyes as if weighing her proposition. 'OK. But don't think because I'm old I'm going to forget about it.'

Tilly laughed. 'Forgetting *anything* is the very last thing that would ever happen to you.'

Through the window Jock could see Tilly and Eunice still chatting away. He'd seen in a research paper that women spoke three times more words in a day than men did. That statistic didn't surprise him in the least, although it did fascinate him. What did they talk about all day? Maybe he should ask them.

No, better not. The discussion looked serious.

He laughed at himself, too afraid of what their answer might be. But he admitted that he found Tilly intriguing—he was more than a little interested in what she might have to say. He'd never met anyone quite like her. As close to an heiress as he'd ever meet, but you'd never guess. He knew plenty of rich people— some of them had inherited wealth and others had made their own money, but he didn't know any who had left all that behind to work in underdeveloped nations. Travel the world and pass through some poor countries, maybe, but not forsake all their comforts for the benefit of others.

She was bright, motivated and down to earth. What had drawn her to foreign aid work? He was curious to know what made her tick. What made her laugh out loud? What moved her? When was she happiest, most at peace? What would her lips taste of if he— He slammed a mental lid shut on that thought. It had become increasingly persistent. He'd found his gaze drawn to her full mouth pursed in sleep once too often on the drive to Cockatoo Gully.

There was no denying he found her attractive. Not beautiful but vibrant. She was too full of spirit to ever go unnoticed and she had legs that went on for ever. He was going to enjoy the next few months, he thought as he pushed open the door.

Kylie was behind the desk, phone held to her ear. He smiled at her and she held up one hand, indicating for him to stop. He pushed thoughts of Tilly aside.

'Jock, wait. Daisy Williams has just delivered her baby but there's a problem.'

He stopped in his tracks. 'With Daisy or the baby?'

'The baby. His colour's not right.'

'Who's with her?'

'Ruthie.'

'OK.' While not a trained midwife, Ruthie was an Aboriginal elder who'd probably delivered more babies than Jock. If she said there was a problem, he believed it. 'Have they cut the cord yet?' He waited as Kylie relayed the question.

'Yep.'

Damn. 'I'm on my way. What's the address?' He listened with one ear as he raced to grab the portable oxygen cylinder and a handful of neonatal masks. 'Tilly!' he yelled in her direction. 'We've got an emergency. Let's go.'

She was waiting, clutching her medical bag, as he came back to the reception area. Good, she was on the ball.

'We'll take the truck. I'll explain on the way.'

He jumped into the four-wheel-drive, assuming Tilly would follow. She did. There was no time for chivalry on this trip. Daisy's baby was his priority now. Shoving the gearstick into first, he pulled into the main street as he started telling Tilly what he knew. Which wasn't much.

'We're just about there. We'll need to start with the baby. Can you take its obs? Ruthie will look after Daisy and we can check her later.'

He stopped in front of a row of identical fibro houses, identical in everything but colour. 'Daisy's is the green one.' They jumped out simultaneously, grabbed their gear and headed for the house.

The front door opened directly into a lounge room, sparsely furnished but neat. No sign of anyone in this room. They found Ruthie, Daisy and the baby in Daisy's bedroom. Ruthie seemed calm enough but Daisy looked to be on the verge of tears. He knew new mums worried about every little thing, even when there was no cause for concern. He could only imagine what must be going through Daisy's mind at the moment when things were obviously not going according to plan.

'Hi, Daisy, Ruthie. This is Dr Tilly.' His introduction was brief. From the sound of things he didn't have time to waste on pleasantries. Daisy was sitting on the edge of the bed, holding the infant. 'How about you let me have a look at your baby while Ruthie looks after you?' He looked at the midwife, inclining his head toward Daisy, suggesting that she help to keep her occupied. Fortunately Ruthie got the message.

Jock gently removed the baby from Daisy's arms, laying it at the foot of the bed to be unwrapped. 'Tell us what's been going on while I have a look at this little man.'

'He was fine until I cut the cord,' Ruthie said. 'Then his colour started to change. He seems a bit flat.'

Jock had to agree with that. Most newborns protested loudly when their warm blankets were removed, this one lay quietly, his little chest rising and falling rapidly but without any other movements.

Once the cord was cut the baby had to breathe on its own. Poor colour was usually indicative of a circulatory problem but colour was a difficult thing to ascertain in Aboriginal babies because of their dark skin. Jock gently pulled down the baby's lower eyelids, checking the skin inside. Definitely paler than it should be. He checked inside the baby's mouth. The mucous membranes were a dark red, a raspberry-like colour, indicating cyanosis. Definitely a circulatory problem.

'Respiration 30 per minute. Heart rate 140.' Tilly's voice broke the silence. The baby's breathing was fast but his heart rate was within normal limits. His poor colour indicated a lack of oxygenated blood reaching the tissues, his rapid breathing perhaps a reaction to this—an attempt to get more oxygen into his system.

'He needs oxygen.'

Tilly had anticipated his request and had the portable oxygen cylinder and masks by his side as he spoke. Jock slipped the tiny mask over the baby's face as Tilly connected the tubing.

'Fifteen litres per minute.' Jock issued instructions as Tilly turned the oxygen on, adjusting the output to give Jock the flow he wanted.

'Can you test oxygen sats and blood pressure?' Jock waited for Tilly to acknowledge his request before grabbing a stethoscope and placing it against the baby's chest wall. He moved it around, listening carefully, certain he would hear a heart murmur. He started at the base of the heart. There was nothing unusual on the right but, then, it was more common to hear a murmur at the left base. Nothing there, either. He moved the stethoscope to the apex of the heart. There it was. A very definite murmur.

He lifted his head to check on Daisy, relieved to see that Ruthie had her distracted with routine obs. She was probably repeating things she'd already done but Jock was grateful. He didn't have time to spend reassuring Daisy at the moment, especially when he couldn't offer much comfort. This baby was in serious trouble.

'Oxygen sats are 82 per cent, BP 100 over 60.' Tilly's voice was a whisper as she read out the reading from the tiny finger probe measuring the baby's oxygen uptake. His blood pressure was OK but his oxygen levels were still too low. 'Any ideas?'

'Septal defect with an apical murmur and cyanosis. He's not getting the oxygen he needs and it's serious. I'm thinking something like transposition of the great vessels.' Both were keeping their voices low so as not to alarm Daisy.

From Tilly's expression, it was obvious that she'd heard of this before and knew the dangers. 'Have you seen this condition before?'

She nodded. 'Only in Indonesia and always at autopsy. We didn't have access to surgeons.' She didn't need to say any more. Without surgery these babies didn't survive. 'What do we do?'

'I'll call the Flying Doctor. He'll have to be evacuated to Brisbane and we'll try to stabilise him as best we can while we wait. Are you happy to start a drip running? He'll need antibiotics and Lasix. I'll ring the Flying Docs from outside.'

Tilly nodded and by the time he returned she had a drip inserted, a bag of saline hooked up and was checking the dosages of the drugs. Jock double-checked her calculations before injecting the drugs into the drip.

'Can you repeat his obs? I need to tell Daisy what's happening.'

'Sure. I'll take care of him.'

Jock looked at the tiny baby, a mask covering his face and tubes coming out of his arm. 'We'll do our best, little one. You'll be OK.' Now he had to speak to Daisy.

'How's it going here?'

'The placenta's delivered. Daisy's fine.' Ruthie's answer was brief and to the point.

'How's my baby, Dr Jock? Is he OK?'

Jock knew he had to deliver the news very carefully. Some good news first before he gave Daisy the facts. But this was easier said than done. There wasn't much good news except that her baby was still alive. 'Dr Tilly is looking after him. He's having difficulty getting oxygen into his body, which is why his colour isn't good. We're giving him oxygen through a mask but he's a very sick little boy, Daisy.'

Daisy had started crying even before Jock had finished his sentence. Ruthie sat on one side of her, stroking her back as Jock sat on the other side and tried to get Daisy to listen.

'Daisy, we are doing everything we can but we'll have to fly you both down to Brisbane. Your baby needs to be in hospital.

You can't stay here.' Daisy's wails increased in volume with this bit of news and Jock didn't have the heart to continue, but he knew he had to inform Daisy about the situation.

'I think there's a problem with his blood vessels and the way they are attached to his heart. I think they might be attached the wrong way around.' His explanation was going to be basic but it would get the idea across if Daisy was listening. He glanced at Ruthie, who nodded her head. *Keep going*, he thought she meant. 'This means that the blood from his lungs, which is carrying the oxygen, is going round in circles back to his lungs instead of to his heart. The heart isn't getting oxygenated blood to pump around the body.'

Daisy went silent—it appeared she had been listening—and then she spoke. 'Did he have this problem before he was born?'

'No. Before the cord was cut he was getting his oxygen directly from you, straight to his heart. Babies' lungs don't really work until they are born. He needs surgery to switch the blood vessels around, get him wired up properly. It's not uncommon to see this and after surgery he should be fine. But we need to get you both to Brisbane. Do you understand?'

Daisy nodded. She gulped. 'Can I hold him?'

Jock looked at Tilly.

'I've done all I can for the moment,' she said.

He knew that Daisy needed to hold her baby, and in all probability the baby needed his mum, too.

Tilly brought the baby to Daisy while Jock repositioned the drip bag and the oxygen cylinder. Daisy lay back on her bed, hugging her baby to her breast, tears in her eyes. There was nothing to do for the moment except wait. But Jock was never any good at passing the time in idleness.

'I'll just check in with the Flying Doctors.' That would fill in a couple of minutes, by which time he could check the baby's obs again. He ducked out of the room.

'They should be here in about ten minutes,' he said as he came back into the bedroom. 'We need to work out the best way of getting Daisy and the baby to the airstrip.' Tilly was standing by the window, not looking at him. He waited for her response. Had she heard him? She didn't reply.

'Tilly? Tilly!'

She was staring off into space. What on earth was she thinking about? Now was not the time for daydreaming.

'Tilly, the plane's about to land. We need to get organised.'

Still no reply. Had she gone into shock? Surely she'd coped with bigger emergencies than this before.

He crossed the room in four paces to stand beside her. He put a hand on her shoulder, trying not to startle her. Her expression was blank and apprehension gripped him. He clasped her shoulder a little tighter and gave it a slight shake. 'Tilly?'

CHAPTER FOUR

'TILLY?'

'Yes?' She jumped at the sound of Jock's voice. He was standing right next to her, his hand on her shoulder. When had he come back into the room?

'Are you OK?'

She blinked. 'Sure. Why?'

'You're standing here with your eyes closed and you didn't respond when I called you. The plane is about to land. We need to get going.' He was looking at her carefully. 'You look a bit pale—sure you're OK?'

'I'm fine.' She looked across the room to where Daisy lay with her baby. Were they OK?

'It's not your headache, is it?'

'No.' She felt a bit disoriented but didn't have a trace of a headache. 'I was just a little light-headed for a second,' she said, her voice a little higher than normal. But she was pretty sure that was because he still hadn't moved his hand from her bare arm and the skin-to-skin contact was nice. Very nice. She leant in a little, to support her claim. 'Maybe I need to check exactly what herbs Kylie put in my tea.'

'Sure that's all it is? Maybe you're coming down with something.'

She shook her head. 'I'm fine. Really. Shall we take their obs again before we transfer them?'

She moved away, out of reach of Jock's touch, so she could think more clearly. She wondered how long she'd been standing still and hoped it hadn't been more than a minute or two.

Tilly started checking the baby, leaving Daisy for Jock. She didn't need to talk to the baby and that left time for her to think. Dizzy spells and headaches. She wasn't normally prone to headaches and the combination of symptoms was beginning to worry her. She remembered her promise to Eunice. She'd have to make the appointment with the foreign aid doctor and have a thorough medical. There were plenty of reasons for her symptoms, most of them minor, but she couldn't afford any mistakes. Not with other people's lives at risk.

She finished checking the baby and breathed a sigh of relief when his heart rate, blood pressure and oxygen sats were all OK. From then on it was a flurry of activity as they organised the transfer and handed the care of their patients over to the Flying Doctors.

Jock came to stand beside her as they watched the small aircraft take off to the north before banking to the east and heading for Brisbane. Tilly self-consciously tried to smooth her hair, knowing she must look a mess, then realised that she had little hope of improving her appearance with just her fingertips. She let her hands drop to her sides.

'Good work today, Tilly. That baby has a good chance of making it, thanks to us.'

'Thanks to you and your quick diagnosis. It seems as if you were spot on.'

'I hope so. It's up to the surgeons now.'

Tilly glanced at her watch. Nearly six. The time had flown by.

'What next?' she asked. 'Is Kylie expecting us back at the clinic?'

Jock shook his head. 'No. When I checked the Flying Docs' ETA I asked Kylie to send everyone home until the morning. I thought we'd be better off making an early start tomorrow rather than heading back to the clinic now. Is that OK with you?'

Tilly had a moment's pause when she wondered if he'd done that for her benefit. But from his wording he'd organised this before her dizzy spell, so it wasn't related. And if he wasn't going to raise that issue, neither was she. 'Perfectly OK with me.'

'Good. Are we still on for dinner?'

She nodded. It was just what she needed, and she'd been looking forward to it for the last two days.

'Seven o'clock too early?'

'I'm famished. Can you make yourself beautiful in half an hour instead?'

He laughed. 'I'd need longer that that, so we'll forget about me. Six-thirty it is. Let's take the car back to the hotel and go from there.'

Twenty minutes later Jock was in the bar of the hotel, waiting for Tilly to shower and change. He checked his watch and assumed Tilly would be a little while yet, it was still ten minutes before the time they'd agreed to meet. He signalled to the barman and ordered a glass of beer.

His sipped his drink while he watched the door and waited. He was glad he'd suggested dinner and even more glad she'd accepted. It had been a long time since he'd asked a woman out to dinner and he'd been concerned he'd asked her too soon, had seemed gauche, but she hadn't seemed to think he was too forward. It had even taken him by surprise, the strong desire to get to know her, to spend time with her away from work.

Getting involved with a woman was something he hadn't been game to do for years. It always seemed to end the same way: with demands for more of him and resentment about the time and energy he'd spent at work and with his two younger siblings. They'd had a point, he knew. There had never been a lot of time left over for relationships and now he was flat out with setting up his pet project, the family unit at the hospital, there was even less.

Despite that, the desire to spend a bit of his limited free time with Tilly had sneaked up on him and he'd acted on it. She was different to any other woman he'd been involved with. For one thing, she was the most independent woman he'd ever been attracted to. Her chosen work was testament to that. He couldn't imagine her getting clingy or complaining about his commitments. If she lived here, she'd probably cram more into a day than him.

The fact that she was only here for the short term removed any risk of things turning out as they always had in the past. It was perhaps the reason why he'd let his guard down and allowed himself to be interested in the first place.

He'd already made it clear he was interested in hearing about her work. Maybe tonight he'd act on his instincts and let her know it was more than just professional curiosity.

Besides, after this afternoon's events he wouldn't have been happy for her to be wandering around on her own so he would've kept an eye on her, anyway. He was just fortunate that it was no hardship, none at all.

He knew of the mix-up at the hospital yesterday when Tilly had kept Adam Davey waiting, but that hadn't overly concerned him. It had only been her first full day on the job. Today was a different story.

He fiddled with the coasters, turning them around to face each chair, squaring them up with the edge of the table, while he ran through the events of the day. He was certain she hadn't told him the whole truth about the episode in Daisy's house. He wondered if it was related to her headaches but without a complete check-up he had no way of knowing. Fortunately there had been no repercussions for their patients. He decided he could afford to adopt a wait-and-see policy, keep an eye on her and hopefully get some answers.

He picked up his glass, lifting his head just in time to see her walk into the bar. She was wearing denim jeans, a cotton shirt knotted at the waist and slip-on flat shoes that looked like they'd seen better days. Her hair was still a little damp from the shower and her skin glowed. She looked good.

In fact, she looked the picture of health and vitality and he wondered again what was going on.

'Been waiting long?' She smiled.

'No, this is my first drink.' She was five minutes early but she didn't look as if she'd rushed. 'Can I get you a drink?'

'Something soft, thanks.'

'Lemon, lime and bitters?'

'Perfect. If you know what you want to eat, we can order. I've had the same thing ever since I first came here with my grandpa as a seven-year-old. Beef burger. Eaten at the front bar while he had a beer with his mates.'

Jock turned to the bar to place their orders, looking back for a moment as he waited for the waitress to find her notepad. Tilly was scanning the room, a smile on her face, relaxed and looking like she didn't have a care in the world. He was no expert but her face looked free of make-up, as it had since they'd met. He wasn't a fan of make-up—from what he'd seen, most women didn't need it. Tilly certainly didn't. Her skin was clear and fresh, her face framed by her dark blonde hair. He'd thought her attractive when they'd first met and he'd been honest when he'd complimented her on her newly cut hair. It did suit her. But for someone so blessed by Mother Nature, she didn't seem to be aware of it. He'd not seen her fussing with her appearance and although she dressed neatly for work, she didn't look like she'd ever consider spending time debating which scarf went with which earrings. It was another trait setting her apart from anyone else he'd ever dated—even his easygoing sister Jules preened more than Tilly seemed to. It had him intrigued. Was she as low-maintenance as she seemed?

He finished ordering and, picking up their drinks, walked to her side, placed a hand lightly beneath her elbow and guided her to a small table on the opposite side of the room. They sat down and he asked, 'Have you still got a headache? Is that why you ordered a soft drink?'

'My headache's gone—the aspirin this morning took care of that.'

She looked and sounded bright enough but he guessed she wasn't one to complain so he went on, 'Are you sure? I saw Eunice holding your head at lunchtime.'

Tilly thought he was pushing their fledgling friendship but she raised one eyebrow and answered anyway. 'She was just picking up where my headache had been. I told her it had gone.'

'Any idea about what brought it on?'

She shrugged. 'I'm still a bit tired. It's been a bit of a whirl-wind—first my grandpa dying, then moving back and starting a new job straight away.'

'I'm sorry about your grandpa. I knew him a little, just as a neighbour. He was a real gentleman. You must miss him.'

'He was and I do. I was lucky to be able to spend time with him last year when he was first diagnosed and then I came back briefly for his funeral, so at least I feel like I got to say a proper goodbye.'

'Can I ask why you've come back now?'

'I promised him I'd come back for a month or so to be with my grandmother after he died. He was worried about her. She doesn't reach out for help very easily.'

'Why did you take the job?'

'I promised to come home, I didn't promise to *stay* at home. Despite what my grandpa wished, my grandmother and I have never been close,' she explained, giving a small shrug.

'Then I take it you're not thinking about moving back here permanently.'

She shook her head emphatically. 'Lord, no. Although every

now and then I need a break from aid work, once I'm here and I see how fortunate everyone is I feel even more strongly about returning overseas where I can really make a difference. I'm not needed here, not in the same way.'

'Your gran, doesn't she need you? Not even now?'

'She's certainly never said as much. She's a pretty strong woman, very self-sufficient. I can't imagine her relying on me any more than she would let me depend on her. It might help her a bit right now, but in the long run she'd never turn to me. I'm only here because I promised Grandpa. If I wasn't working, Gran and I would drive each other mad within a week.'

He looked like he was fighting to suppress a smile but he failed. 'So it's your grandmother giving you headaches.'

She laughed and said, 'Things aren't that bad between us—we'll just never be the best of friends.'

'If it's not your grandmother, have you checked your BP?'

'Yes. It's fine.'

'What about your electrolytes? Do you want me to do a blood test?'

He was raising all the questions that had been running through her mind but she didn't want to discuss her health. 'Relax, Jock.' She tried to make light of it, wanting him to forget about it and get their evening back on track. 'It was just a headache. It's nothing.'

The look on his face said he still wasn't convinced.

'I have to schedule an appointment in Brisbane some time for a medical. It's a routine thing at the end of an overseas placement. We're all meant to have a medical when we return from a posting but they didn't have an appointment free in the few days I had before I started work. They'll do all the standard checks.' There. Hopefully that would buy her a reprieve. 'Honestly, I'm not just saying it—I feel fine.'

'I'm driving down to the city on Friday. I have a morning meeting about government funding for the family unit. Why don't you see if you can get an appointment then and come with me?'

'What about work?'

'There's a clinic at Emerald Downs every fortnight, but that's next week, so your diary will be clear.'

'I doubt they'd be able to fit me in at such short notice.' She was making excuses without really knowing why, and Jock seemed to recognise her stalling tactics.

'Why don't I ring for you, pull a few strings?'

'I can do it, Jock, and I *will* do it when I get a moment.'

'I like to help.' He shrugged, looking sheepish. 'Bad habit.'

'I know you're just trying to help, and thanks, but it's fine.' Tilly picked up her drink, turning her attention to stirring it in a blatant attempt to end that subject. Would he comment on her abrupt change of topic? She was convinced she was just over-tired and had had too much to deal with. It was quite a list, by anyone's standards.

The waitress brought their plates, piled high with food in true country-pub fashion. Jock, between bites, asked, his voice teasing, 'Have you always been so independent?'

As her mouth was full, she couldn't answer, so she scowled at him, only half-joking.

He held up his hands, seeming to protest he'd meant well. 'Hey, I'm not saying it's a bad thing. Quite the opposite.'

She took him at his word and relaxed, accepting he wasn't being critical. 'Sorry if I jumped on you. I'm sensitive to people criticising me for being too independent or not settling down. I get it a lot whenever I'm out of the field and I don't like it. I don't come home and start lecturing people to go do aid work and I don't get why they do it to me.'

'They probably feel threatened.'

'Why?' Her surprise was clear in the tone of her voice.

'When someone does things very differently, it highlights how others are choosing to live their lives. Some people don't like what they see as a result and they want you to change so they don't have to feel uncomfortable.'

'But I don't think they're jealous.'

'They're not necessarily, although I'm sure some are. It's more that most of us cruise around in our own comfort zone. When we come into contact with something or someone that challenges our way of doing things, a common reaction is to reject it or try and control it.'

'Oh.' She sat for a moment without speaking, mulling over his suggested explanation. It seemed plausible, good even.

'I'll send the account on to you,' he joked, bringing her thoughts back to him.

She pretended to shudder. 'I'm afraid to ask how much. I don't think I can afford the psychoanalyst you've turned out to be.'

'Then I'll take a break and you can tell me how you got to be so good at standing on your own two feet.'

'My grandmother.' The instantaneousness of her answer surprised even her and she felt her mouth forming an O of surprise. 'Excuse me while I have another light-bulb moment,' she said, laughing. 'I've never really thought about how I got to be this way. I always assumed I was born independent and that going off to boarding school sealed my fate. But now I think about it, growing up under the care of the most independent woman I've ever met would mean even a shrinking violet would be able to manage on her own.'

Jock threw back his head and laughed. Tilly found herself joining in, his laughter infectious. 'Tilly, I haven't known you for long, but I do know that, strong grandmother or not, you were never destined to be a shrinking violet.'

'Probably not, but, like I said, Gran would've stamped that out of me long ago anyway. My independence is the only thing she's ever seemed accepting of.'

'Why would that be?'

'Probably because it made me the very opposite of my mum, who she didn't get on with at all.' Tilly put her cutlery down, clasped her hands under her chin, and held Jock's gaze, schooling her features into the picture of seriousness. 'Jock, you are causing me to have entirely too many personal insights for one evening. You wanted me to regale you with witty travel anecdotes, I thought, not bore you with self-analysis.'

'I need the self-analysis to help me understand the grown-up Tilly, who goes places where she can collect witty anecdotes,' he responded. 'So,' he said, leaning back in his chair and adopting the sombre tone of a therapist, 'let me take you back further in time. Tell me about boarding school. How old were you when you went?'

'Fourteen.' She laughed, answering despite her attempt to change the subject away from her personal history.

Jock nodded in a knowing way. 'Ah, the age when girls become a handful.'

'I was a model child,' she protested, still smiling. 'What makes you think I was a handful?'

'I can only think that a woman with a will and mind as resolute as yours would've been a handful from a toddler.'

She looked at him, trying to see which angle he was coming from. He caught her look and grinned. 'In a good way,' he continued in his normal voice.

She frowned at him, teasing, 'I've been nothing but angelic since you met me.' It was true, too, she reflected. Almost true. Her thoughts about him hadn't been exactly angelic but he didn't know about that.

'They're always the ones you have to watch out for.' He winked at her and then, oblivious to the fact his wink had just turned her insides to mush, glanced at her plate and said, 'Looks like your beef burger is good.'

His own plate was empty, he'd eaten every last crumb.

'Superb. Did you want to try some? I could never finish my dinner here as a child and I'm still struggling.'

'Did you come here a lot?'

'Not that often for dinner. But I'd come into town with my

grandpa for cattle auctions or he'd bring me here if Gran was at a CWA meeting. I used to sit at the bar with a packet of chips and a lemonade and pretend to be grown-up. And when I got bored I'd go off and play with Johnny.'

'Interesting.' Jock dragged the word out. 'Who was he?'

'The publican's son.' She paused while their plates were removed. 'He was the first boy I kissed.'

'Now I'm really interested. How old were you?'

'Thirteen.' She spooned sugar into her coffee, stirring it. 'He was fifteen.'

'Ah, an older man. No wonder you were packed off to boarding school. So what was it like? Did he set a high standard?'

'Not at all. It was over so fast I didn't even have time to shut my eyes.'

'I hope a few of us males have made up for Johnny's shortcomings since.'

Tilly smiled as she sipped her drink. 'He was sweet.'

Jock laughed. 'That's as much a kiss-off as saying he had a good personality.'

'He *was* sweet.' She stared off into the distance, pretending to reminisce. 'Ah, I wonder what happened to him.'

'You lost touch with your first love?'

'He wasn't my first love, he was the first boy I kissed. Big difference.' Tilly could see the question in Jock's eyes. 'Don't think I'm about to spill those beans tonight, too. I've given you quite enough information. Way too much, in fact.'

'Spoilsport.'

'And unless you're going to share any of your deep dark secrets with me, I think I might hit the sack.' She waited but Jock didn't take up her offer.

'My stories will keep for another night. But next time we have dinner it's still your turn. I still haven't heard about your work and my stories will come a pale second.'

'I don't believe that for a second.' Tilly kept her voice light but she felt like doing a happy little dance. He wanted to have dinner with her again!

With an effort she did as Jock did and pushed back her chair with no break in decorum, rising and walking beside him out of the bar. But on the inside she indulged in a mental happy dance instead.

Their accommodation was on the first floor and as they passed the space under the stairs she couldn't resist adding another snippet of information, still buzzing with the knowledge he wanted to spend another evening with her. She pointed under the stairs. 'That's where he kissed me.'

He stooped immediately and turned her to face him. 'Where?'

'Here, under the stairs. This used to have a curtain over it. Mr Bernardi used to store stuff in here and we used it as a cubby-house.'

'No.' His voice was quieter, caressing. 'I meant where did he kiss *you*?'

'Oh.' Tilly gulped as the air between them seemed to warm and crackle to life, all thoughts of Johnny Bernardi banished so that it was an effort to remember the answer to his question. 'Here.' Tilly touched her fingers to her lips. She saw Jock's eyes follow her hand, saw his eyes darken to slate grey as he watched her touch her mouth. She breathed deeply as he took one step to close the distance between them.

He was standing just a few inches from her now and she had to tilt her head up to meet his gaze. She held her breath as he reached forward, placing his fingers under her chin, tipping her head up further.

'Thank you for joining me for dinner.'

She let her breath out, disappointed he hadn't kissed her when she'd been sure he'd been about to do just that. 'My pleasure.'

But his fingers were still resting on her face and, mesmerised, she felt, more than watched, as he leant forward, oh, so slowly. When he was so close her vision became blurred, she closed her eyes, the anticipation achingly painful. When the soft touch of his mouth brushed against hers, her lips parted slightly, involuntarily, sending shivers of excitement through her body. He deepened the kiss, but only by a tiny, teasing touch, leaving her torn between an exquisite ache to have this lovely, perfect kiss never end and a desire for him to pull her against him and kiss her with an intensity that would send every rational thought from her brain.

He moved his mouth over hers and she sank into him a little, her only thought being that this kiss was quite simply one that could curl a woman's toes—any woman's—in just the right way. And she breathed a little sigh of satisfaction that she was that woman, but the satisfaction was over too soon.

He pulled gently back, and said, 'Thanks for your company.'

When she opened her eyes, she found him smiling at her. He looked pleased with himself. With good reason, she thought. He didn't seem to doubt the effect he had on her but it didn't seem smug, more like he was happy with the event. In which case, the feeling was mutual.

'I'll see you in the morning,' he continued, his voice low and gravelly, the only clue that he was as shaken up as her.

'See you then,' she replied when she'd recovered her power of speech. Their evening was obviously at an end, albeit it had been a happy one. She recovered the power of movement next and walked the few steps to the bottom of the stairs.

'Sleep tight,' he called as she ascended the stairs. His voice was soft in the quiet of the hallway, winding its way around her, almost making her go back down to him, so strong was its pull. 'Don't let the bed bugs bite.'

The spell ended. 'There aren't any!' she protested, and he chuckled.

'No, I just couldn't resist.'

He was still laughing softly when she reached the landing and raised a hand in farewell, before she headed up the next flight of stairs and he disappeared from view.

So long, Johnny Bernardi, she thought as she reached her room and stood for a moment, key in hand. She had other memories of the Commercial Hotel now and they were a definite improvement.

Thursday morning was glorious, clear blue skies and the promise of another perfect warm day. Not too humid for this time of year, which suited Tilly. Despite having enjoyed the best 'first kiss' of her life last night, she'd slept soundly and didn't have a trace of a headache this morning. Actually, it was probably because of that kiss, not in spite of it, she thought as she got herself ready for the next patient. The day had been so busy already, catching up on everyone who'd missed out on the clinic the day before, she hadn't even had a chance to speak privately with Jock yet. She was about to call in her next patient when the door opened and Jock walked in.

She really didn't have time to spare, but she found herself not caring and her smile was immediate when she saw it was him. 'You look like the cat that got the cream.'

'The whole saucer.' He grinned, and for some reason she found herself thinking about how they'd first met and how little she'd been wearing, and she felt a tinge of red steal across her cheeks.

'Then you're a greedy little feline.'

'Greedy for more. But…' he shook his head, adopting an expression of such woebegone misery that she laughed '…now is unfortunately neither the time nor the place. I just wanted to check how you're feeling today. Also,' he said, leaning against the doorframe, 'at the risk of offending Little Miss Independent—and remember…' he held up his hands as she went to speak '…I mean that in a *good* way—I wanted to check if you've managed to make that appointment with your doctor.'

'I'm feeling excellent, thanks for asking, Dr Kelly,' she teased.

'And when I have two minutes free from unnecessary interruptions, I'll make that call.'

His grin was pure cheek. 'Ah, that would be me you're referring to. I'll let you get on with things.' He straightened up and started to walk away, then turned back to her. 'But if you start feeling unwell, let me know. I mean that. I may have ravished you under the stairs last night, but I'm still your boss.'

With a wink he slipped out of the room and closed the door, leaving her spluttering with laughter and not quite able to believe what he'd just said. She shook her head as she headed for the door, muttering to herself as she went, 'And I'm meant to act like the cool, calm, collected doctor for the rest of the day *how* exactly?'

She heard Jock and caught glimpses of him during the rest of the day but not to speak to, their busy lists leaving them no more spare, snatched minutes. She'd been lucky to find the time to phone the Royal Brisbane Hospital, but she'd promised Jock that she would and she knew he'd check on her again.

As it was, she'd managed to persuade them to squeeze her in for an appointment the following day and breezed through the afternoon without any dramas.

By the time Jock finally knocked on her door, just as she'd finished with her last patient, she was starting to feel weary. But the prospect of the drive home with him brought with it a second wind and she found herself offering to drive.

Once in the car, they slipped into chatting in such an easy way she'd never have believed they barely knew each other. Then again, she'd never have believed he'd have kissed her already either. There was no awkwardness. He seemed as comfortable in her company as she was in his, and she relaxed in the knowledge.

'How was it, working in your old town with all the old familiar faces?' he asked once they had left Cockatoo Gully and were driving through the open plains which would, in an hour or so, climb into the mountains behind Noosa.

'Not as many familiar faces as I'd expected.'

'Ah, Johnny Bernardi didn't show up.' Tilly laughed and swatted him lightly on the arm as he went on, 'Any other old boyfriends?'

'That's confidential.'

'I don't expect you to tell me names, just numbers,' Jock teased. 'How many broken hearts did you have to fix?'

'Two.' She paused for a fraction of a second. 'But once I told them you weren't worth crying over, they recovered pretty quickly.'

'*Touché.*' Jock raised one eyebrow and inclined his head a little in her direction.

'Enough about me.' It was the second time she'd said that to him in the last two days. He seemed to have a talent for steering the conversation away from himself. 'What happened to the first girl you kissed?'

'I proposed to her.'

'You what?' Tilly's jaw dropped.

'Yep.' Jock grinned. 'I fell for her the day we met. Ah, Suzanne. She was tiny and blonde.' Tilly quelled a shiver of jealousy. 'We were at kindergarten, we were four.' He was laughing now, they both were. 'Took me two years to work up to kissing her. I obviously wasn't as game as good old Johnny.' Tilly poked him in the ribs. 'And then I invited our parents to come for dinner when we got married.'

'I take it you didn't do the "happily ever after" thing. What happened?'

'I turned seven and had no time for girls. But she still holds the record for my longest relationship—three years!'

Tilly joined in the laughter. The tension she'd half expected to rise between them since their kiss hadn't eventuated. They'd fallen into an easy, teasing conversation. Perhaps on this drive she'd learn a bit more about Jock Kelly.

Her plans were short-lived. Jock closed the subject, and all others, by pulling his Akubra hat over his eyes, putting his head back and falling asleep. Tilly drove the rest of the way singing along to the radio, but it didn't disturb Jock's slumber.

Still, she reflected as she took the turn back into Noosa, they'd have another two-hour drive to Brisbane tomorrow. Just the two of them, in the car, with nothing to do but talk. She'd save her questions for then.

CHAPTER FIVE

WHAT was that quote about best-laid plans? Tilly mused as she rubbed her head the next morning, one hour into the drive to Brisbane. She'd felt the headache start up again almost as soon as they'd left Noosa. She'd been perfectly fine for almost two days, while they'd been at Daisy's, and she'd managed to convince both herself and Jock her symptoms were simply due to fatigue.

She didn't want to start looking like a hypochondriac and take a tablet in front of him, so she persevered, gritting her teeth every time the car hit a bump in the road and trying to hold a normal conversation despite the fact her head felt like it was going to explode.

She did her best to chat but the easy camaraderie of the previous day had gone. There was no denying her conversation was far from scintillating and he seemed less attentive than usual. By the time Jock dropped her off at the Royal Brisbane Hospital he must have been convinced she was either boring or exhausted. It shouldn't matter, but it did, she thought as she walked through the hospital, looking for the signs that would lead her to the right department.

It had taken her a while to navigate the map in the entrance foyer and then transfer that information to the actual buildings. The hospital was on a massive scale compared to Noosa and the tropical diseases department was tucked away in a corner of a hospital so convoluted that to say it was like a rabbit warren would be a compliment. Still, she'd made it and was sitting in the consultant's office, going through the standard return assessment, chatting generally about her time overseas and doing her best to summon up the courage to admit to the symptoms that had been increasingly bothering her.

The consultant, Andrea Jones, had taken her blood pressure, height, weight, pulse, checked reflexes and eyesight, all the usual things, and nothing appeared out of the ordinary. Now she was selecting various tubes she'd need for blood tests and Tilly was persuaded into action—no point waiting until the needle was out of her arm before telling Andrea about her symptoms. The needle would be going straight back in again to draw blood for more specific tests.

Andrea moved to Tilly's side and Tilly shoved her sleeve up above her elbow, extending her arm to allow the tourniquet to be fitted.

'I should tell you I've had some symptoms over the last month or so. I thought it was probably due to me needing a break, but if anything they've increased since I've been home.'

Andrea stopped tightening the cuff around Tilly's upper arm. 'Tell me about them.'

Tilly shrugged. She'd managed to convince herself so well that nothing was wrong, she found she really didn't want to talk about it. Though as a medico, she knew it had to be done. She also knew she should have made it a priority to have this check-up as soon as she had got back to Noosa, even without any symptoms, but she'd never been one to easily admit something was wrong.

'Persistent, recurring headaches.' She indicated the location on her head. 'And I seem to be forgetting things.' She was watching Andrea's face for any tell-tale signs that Andrea was worried or had an inkling of what was wrong with her, but the woman's face was impassive.

'What sort of things?'

'Everyday things. Things other people would write notes to remind themselves to do but I've never needed to. Now I'm starting to think it might be a good idea. Just to jog my memory.'

'Your blood pressure is fine. Could be low blood sugar levels. Any infection or illness in the last year or so?'

'No.' She shrugged. 'A common cold, a twisted ankle, a dose of giardiasis that responded to Fasigyn. Nothing else.'

'Have you taken any medication for the headaches?'

'Painkillers and or anti-inflammatories. The anti-inflammatories seem to work best.'

'The headaches are one-sided?'

Tilly nodded. 'Always on the left.'

'No visual disturbances, nausea, sensitivity to noise?'

'No, nothing like that at all. It's just pain and I find it difficult to concentrate. It can feel as if my head's about to explode and I don't like sudden movements but I've had none of the other symptoms except for an episode two days ago when I blacked out.'

'Did you faint?'

Tilly shook her head. 'No, from what I can work out, I just went blank for a moment or two, literally just seconds, and then I was fine. That's about all I know and it hasn't happened again.'

'You were in Indonesia for two years, is that right?' Tilly nodded. 'Where were you before that?'

'I spent three years in various parts of the Indian subcontinent. A few trips back here for a couple of months between some of my postings.'

'No health problems in that time?'

'Nothing that jumps out at me. A few nasty bouts of gastro-enteritis that are better left undescribed.' She grimaced. 'And the usual diarrhoea when I went somewhere new. My stomach is pretty much made of cast iron, though. I'm usually the envy of the others, having the local ice in my drinks within the first week of settling in somewhere new, eating from the street stalls.'

'I'm surprised you've lasted this long in that case.'

'Not at all. I'm not silly about it and I'm convinced that it's best to eat where there are lots of locals—that means quick turnover of food, and food that the cooks are skilled at preparing. The worst stomach upset I ever had was after eating at a supposedly Western restaurant. They didn't know how to prepare the food.' She rubbed her abdomen in memory. 'It showed.'

Andrea labelled two specimen jars. 'I'll need a urine sample and a stool sample to test for intestinal bugs, but that's unlikely to be causing these most recent symptoms. If you can give me a urine sample today, you can take the other one with you. These are routine tests for medics returning from overseas. Your recent symptoms are more than likely something viral. Blood tests might indicate something.'

Andrea wrote labels for the test tubes then tightened the tourniquet. She flicked a vein in Tilly's arm and slipped the needle in. Tilly jumped a little and pinched herself on the hand to distract herself from the slight pinch of pain from the needle. A silly technique, but she'd done it since she'd been a child and it worked.

She looked away as Andrea filled five tubes consecutively with her blood, placing each one on a small rack before selecting the next. Other people's blood was fine—hers she didn't need to see.

Sliding the needle out, Andrea pressed a cotton pad down and secured it with a piece of tape. 'If you haven't had any illnesses, what about accidents? Knocks to the head, that sort of thing.'

Tilly sat for a moment. 'I was in a car accident about six or eight weeks before I came home. Nothing serious, though. A car didn't give way at a crossroad, hit us on our left, but it was a low-speed impact.'

'So no immediate symptoms, nothing over the next seventy-two hours?'

Tilly shook her head.

'When did the headaches start, before or after the car accident?'

Tilly thought for a moment. 'I often wonder how patients can't answer simple questions but it's actually hard to remember all the details. I think maybe after.' She thought back through the months since the car crash, trying to picture herself at work. When had it started? She couldn't recall. 'Sorry to be so vague.'

'That's OK. I'll request a cervical X-ray when you have the lung X-ray.' Tilly had known about the latter one, it was routine. 'Just in case you've done something to your neck. But if you haven't had any neck pain or stiffness, I suspect it's probably viral. Don't quote me on that—these things can be hard to get to the bottom of when you've been in remote places, picking up all sorts of exotic memorabilia.'

Tilly grimaced. 'That's memorabilia I could do without.'

'Let me check your glands and your cervical spine.' Andrea palpated the glands in Tilly's neck. 'Nothing significant there. Can you lie on the bed on your tummy while I check your neck?'

Tilly lay down, resting her head on her hands as Andrea palpated the vertebrae in her neck.

'Any tenderness anywhere?'

'No, it all feels fine.'

Andrea pulled out her chair. 'You can sit up. It all feels fine but I'll include the neck X-ray just to be on the safe side.' She sat to write the X-ray orders. 'Unfortunately, a significant percentage of you return with something to remember your overseas odysseys by. Still, keeps me in a job.'

'Glad to oblige.'

'We'll sort you out. Might just take a while to follow the leads.'

'Am I fine to work?'

Andrea pushed the papers over to Tilly and leant back in her chair, tapping her fingertips together. Her gaze was on Tilly but she seemed to be looking beyond her. 'Are you doing surgery or any procedures requiring high precision or quick reflexes?'

Tilly shook her head. 'Nothing like that. Just outpatient clinics.'

'I can't see a problem with that. What about driving? If you're not getting any warning and you experience another blackout, that could be a problem.'

Tilly dropped her gaze. 'I'm not safe?'

'The lack of warning concerns me. I'd recommend no driving until we get to the bottom of this. Something's going on and we'd better find out what. Did you drive here today?'

'I got a lift.'

Andrea nodded. 'Good. Do you have to drive to do your job?'

'I'm doing some remote clinics, the next one is next Wednesday.'

'The test results should be back before then. Let's see what they find and we can make a decision then. Is that OK with you?'

Tilly nodded.

'I'll ring you as soon as the results come back. Can you leave the urine sample with the nurse?'

'Sure. Thanks for fitting me in today.'

'No problem. The sooner we clear this up for you, the better. I'll talk to you soon.'

Tilly felt much happier walking out of the consultation than she had walking in. Andrea seemed to be leaning towards a viral cause and, as long as they could identify the virus, Tilly didn't expect a major problem. Rest and healthy living should do the trick, like she'd thought. And maybe her symptoms weren't worsening—maybe she was just paying more attention to them.

The next problem was Jock. He was bound to ask for an update. She'd simply tell him that her vital signs were all fine and she was waiting on test results for a viral infection. She was sure he'd be happy with her answer. In the short term at least. She'd deal with any other problems once she had the results.

She checked her watch as she stopped in front of the map-board. An hour and a half until she'd arranged to meet Jock back at the car. As long as they were running on time in Radiology, she should still have just enough time after her cervical and lung X-rays to drop in on Daisy and her baby and see how both had been doing since they had been airlifted from Cockatoo Gully. She checked the hospital plan. Paediatrics was on the floor above Radiology, so that was easy enough.

She swallowed two anti-inflammatory tablets, hoping to eradicate her headache before the trip back to Noosa so she'd be able to enjoy Jock's company. Now she knew she was most likely just suffering from a virus or a neck strain, she could put her health out of her mind for now. By early next week she'd know which it was for sure and she'd be on the way to full health again. Then she'd really be free to spend time with Jock with nothing troubling her.

Nothing other than the question of what she wanted to do with the rest of her working life. She was only on three months' leave, but she'd known when she'd come back feeling so tired that it might be time for a change. She just had no idea what other work and lifestyle could give her the same feeling of doing something of value with her life. But that issue, she reflected as she headed for the lift, could wait for a while. For the first time ever, she just wanted to pretend her life was predictable, just as everyone else's seemed to be. She smiled to herself as she admitted what she really meant by that: she wanted to spend some uncomplicated time in Jock's company without any soul-searching or feeling driven to devote herself to higher causes. She'd given herself three months to spend with Gran and now it had turned into one of the nicest presents she'd ever given herself. She'd earned a break. Surely even her gran would agree with that.

So now she had three months to be with Jock, assuming he was willing. And, fingers crossed, that meant three months worth of dissolving under his sigh-inducing kisses.

Tilly hadn't been her usual chatty self on the drive down, but that might have been because she'd tuned into his distraction—his mind had mostly been on his own appointment. A lot hinged on it and he had a bad feeling in his gut, a feeling that had been niggling with increasing insistence at him over the last couple of weeks. He'd been waiting for signed documents to come back from the Department of Health and despite numerous phone calls and emails he'd not received any encouraging replies. Either someone along the line was slack or incompetent or he was being given the run-around, leading up to the big brush-off.

He grimaced as he thought back to the promising start to negotiations and the quick decline after the government's front-bench shuffle. A new health minister, someone by the name of Brad Laurie, had been appointed, and none of Jock's attempts to contact him had elicited any response. Worse than that, in the three weeks since the new appointment, the promised paper-work, granting funding for the unit, hadn't materialised.

Jock was tired of being given the run-around and had finally managed to convince Brad's chief of staff to book him a meeting with the minister. This Brad Laurie had better be ready.

He glanced at his watch to confirm what he already knew—he'd been sitting here twiddling his thumbs for close to half an hour. He was now convinced of the worst: Brad had no intention of meeting him and the deal had been sunk without a trace.

Just as he was about to storm the offices himself, a staff member appeared to show him into the inner sanctum, dispelling his fear that Brad was going to be a no-show. But he knew he'd been right about his second concern when he saw the self-satisfied expression on the minister's face.

Brad only half stood to shake Jock's hand and Jock clenched his teeth at the arrogance of the gesture. Jock got straight to the business at hand, tired of waiting for action. 'I've been disappointed not to receive the papers. It's been like cracking the entry code for the Pentagon to get hold of you and see when I could expect them.'

Brad feigned ignorance. 'I'm not sure what you would've been expecting. A deal hadn't been ironed out. Minister Shelley left it on the basis it needed further consideration. You understand—' his voice took on tones of lofty morality '—I can't snap my fingers to get funding for every project that lands on my desk.' He spread his hands out, inviting Jock to agree and drop the issue.

Jock had expected this—lies, incompetence and self-importance—but he still had a hard time containing his anger. 'When Minister Shelley and I spoke, it was left on the basis that funding was guaranteed for the equipment I needed. All that was left was for the paperwork to be sent through.' He steadied himself for a moment mentally—if he blew his top, this politician would take great delight in showing him the door. And there would be little he himself could do other than lobby the media to apply pressure, a non-confidence-inspiring option if ever there was one. He had to stay on point. Should he refer to his copious notes of the relevant discussion with the previous minister, or would that basically infer Brad was a liar? Which he was—but he was a liar in a position with a lot of power. And that was something Jock was learning had the capacity to make him feel sick to his stomach. 'Let's backtrack and make sure of what we're both talking about. Minister Shelley and I came to an agreement in principle about funding. It was all ironed out.'

Brad interrupted. 'Nothing's ever "all ironed-out".' His voice dripped with sarcasm. 'Until the ink is dry. Unfortunately, there's no money in the budget for your hospital. You can resubmit your request but—'

Jock saw red. 'There was money and it was promised to our new unit!'

'There was money for health care in the budget, yes. But there are other hospitals in Queensland, Dr Kelly, and the money has been allocated elsewhere.'

'Where exactly? Can you tell me that?'

'Toomwarra General.'

'Let me guess.' Jock was furious by now. 'Toomwarra is in your electoral district.'

Brad's silence confirmed his suspicions. He spent the next five minutes using every non-confrontational approach he had in his armoury to try to persuade Brad from his position. Nothing worked and he could see his hopes for the unit evaporating into the ether. No equipment meant no unit. QED. End of story. And that was a scenario he wasn't prepared to contemplate.

'Noosa General needs that unit, Minister Laurie, and we need those funds. You'll be hearing from me again, you can count on it.'

Jock was having a hard time remembering when he'd last been so livid. He knew he was no match in these power games for men who had played them all their careers. He was a doctor, not a businessman, and he would never be a politician. His word was as good as a signed deal—he knew the world didn't work that way but the blatant dishonesty he'd been treated to just now still came as a shock. After half an hour of striding up and down Brisbane's city streets, he was still steaming but he knew he had to rid himself of the feelings before he could sit behind the wheel for the trip back to Noosa. He wouldn't be safe driving like this and he didn't want to inflict such poor company on Tilly.

If not for Tilly meeting him in ten minutes, he'd have gone for a swim to power away his frustration. Brad had kept him waiting so long he'd not ended up with enough time to accomplish any of the matters he'd planned for today. He chalked up another black mark against Brad's name.

He strode back to the car park, halfway between State Parliament and the hospital, and climbed the stairs two at a time, fighting to get his anger under control. When he exited the stairwell he had the first pleasant sensation of the afternoon when he saw Tilly emerge from the lift. Some of the strains of the day dissolved in that instant. When she turned and saw him, a huge smile lit up her face, unravelling a few more knots in his abdomen and bringing the first smile to his own face since earlier that day.

He covered the distance to her side in a few paces. It was an automatic gesture to put his hand on the small of her back and guide her towards his car. 'How was your appointment?'

She shrugged as they fell into step. 'OK. Andrea thinks my symptoms are probably viral. We all come back from the field at some stage with something minor wrong. Seems it's my turn.'

'What are the other possibilities?'

'A neck injury from an MVA I was in a while back.'

They'd reached the car and he dug in his pocket for his keys, pressing the button to unlock her door and reaching to open it.

He waited until they were both in the car, seat belts on, and he'd reversed before he spoke again. 'What's your hunch?'

'Either sounds feasible. I don't usually succumb to bugs so maybe it's my neck.'

Was she telling the truth? He didn't know her well enough yet to be able to read her body language, but he thought he'd detected a slight defiance creep into her voice with her words.

They'd left the car park, and he was navigating the city traffic so he couldn't watch her face or posture any more to even try and guess at any unspoken information.

'Either way, I'm not worried. Andrea has it under control and she'll let me know early next week when the test results start coming in.'

'Fair enough.' He flicked his indicator on and moved into the lane he'd need to take him to the northern freeway. 'What did she say about work?'

The tension in the car picked up before she answered. 'She thought it was OK for me to continue with outpatient clinics.' Jock looked sideways at her but couldn't read anything more into her words. 'I wouldn't put my patients at risk. I would never keep working if I thought I couldn't manage it and I'd never go against my doctor's orders. I won't drive until Andrea gives me the all-clear. That won't interfere with clinic because I'm expecting an easy answer and a quick solution.'

Jock nodded. He was relieved she seemed to be taking a

sensible approach and was thinking of her own health and that of her patients. She was so independent he hadn't been sure how she'd take it if her doctor had scaled back her work options, but she seemed to be accepting it even if it did grate on her.

'So, enough about me. How did your meeting go? Did you get the funding?'

He felt the muscles in his jaw tightening as his mind turned back to his own immediate problems. 'No. It seems as though the funds have been allocated elsewhere.'

'You're not serious?'

'Unfortunately I am. And if my suspicions are correct, the money appears to be going into the minister's electorate.'

'But that money was promised to you, wasn't it?'

Jock nodded. 'Before the unit was even started. I wouldn't have gone ahead otherwise. There's enough we had to raise funds for without paying for hospital equipment that should be government-funded. But this is one fight I won't give up on.'

'What are you going to do?'

'As much as it goes against the grain, I think I'll take the story to the media. It's just the sort of thing they love—government short-changing the health sector. I'm hoping the thought of all that bad press might cause the minister to honour his promise.'

'I'm happy to help. I love a good cause and the unit is just that. The newspapers will love the story.'

'I hope so. At the moment I can't think of any other option.'

She glanced over at him and she could see the muscles in his jaw bulging as he clenched his teeth.

'You'll have a headache like mine by the time we get home if you keep that up.'

He caught her gaze for a moment. 'Come again?'

'Your jaw's as tight as a fist.'

He rubbed at his face briefly and worked his jaw from side to side, easing the tension. 'It's been quite a day.'

'Would you like me to help you relax?' Tilly decided it was time for some levity. Their conversation had been too serious and he clearly felt as little inclined to dwell on the funding issues as she was to discuss her health.

'That's an idea.' His smile was more relaxed this time but she thought she detected an effort on his part to adopt a lighter tone. 'Although I'm not sure how easy it will be, not if you're thinking of long, lazy hours basking in the sun somewhere. Drive me mad.'

She laughed. 'You're probably right, you'd need remedial classes before you could even begin to kick back and do nothing.' She was watching him—wondering how he would react if she pushed a little harder. 'But what about something a little more arduous, a little less resort pace?'

'Rock-climbing? Cross-country running?' Tilly had a moment of self-satisfaction that he hadn't dismissed her suggestion. Seemed like he, too, was keen for them to spend more time together. She hadn't been sure after the drive into Brisbane this morning. 'Scuba?'

Tilly shuddered. 'No deep-sea activities for me. I'm terrified of sharks.'

This time he was surprised and he glanced at her. 'Really?'

'One hundred percent, bona fide terrified.'

'Really?'

She ran her index fingers in a cross on her chest. 'Truly. And rule out any thoughts of getting me to overcome my fear. I'm taking it to the grave with me.'

'Not game to tackle your neuroses?' He was laughing again.

'I'm perfectly happy as I am and I believe phobia would be the correct term, *Dr* Kelly. Except that in my case my fear is not a phobia, it's perfectly rational. You're the insane one, hanging out with giant-fanged fish, begging to be eaten.'

'Not exactly begging, more like being happiest in denial.'

'Maybe we all are, about different things. But as for tomorrow, I was thinking of a walk through the national park. I love it there and I've only been once since I've got back.' She wasn't sure she was up to the more strenuous activities he'd suggested. A pity, because under normal circumstances she was an outdoors girl through and through—as long as it didn't involve a risk of encountering sharks—and she would've liked to have shown him that side of herself. Soon. Hopefully soon. 'Or we could hit the Eumundi markets.'

It was his turn to shudder. 'You'd have to try diving if you wanted me to brave the markets. Browsing with no aim in mind whatsoever is my idea of hell on earth.'

'You're such a bloke.' She caught his gaze and he puffed out his chest in an impersonation of an iron-man. She shook her head. 'And I don't mean that in a positive way.'

He laughed and the atmosphere in the car lost the final touch of tension. 'A walk in the national park is fine by me.' He glanced at her again, eyes narrowed. 'Sure you're up to it?'

'I'm fine. It's just what I need.'

They chatted some more, Tilly telling him about some of the more unusual and funnier experiences she'd had in her overseas postings, Jock responding with some stories of his own. It was late afternoon by the time they approached Noosa. They'd made no plans for that night and Tilly wasn't ready to say goodbye, not now that they'd re-established some of the usual easiness between them. She wouldn't have predicted that, given how stressed he'd been at the beginning of the drive, but they'd been laughing for the last half-hour as they'd swapped funny work stories accrued over the years and she wasn't ready to have the new intimacy come to an end.

'Are you free tonight?'

He looked at her with a quizzical expression masking the mischief in his eyes. 'Asking me on a hot date, Dr Watson?'

'A date, yes.' She kept her expression neutral. 'Not sure how hot it'd be.' She touched her temple. 'I feel a headache coming on.' The grin that had been threatening lit up her face.

The rich sound of his laughter filled the car. 'You've a unique line in passion-killers, I'll give you that.'

'That's a relief.' She kept her face straight with an effort. 'I hate having to pack contraception for a night out.'

He shook his head at her. 'I can see I'm the responsible one here. And the less direct one, too, perhaps.'

'I'm sort of joking.' He didn't need to know she'd been imagining going to bed with him since he'd kissed her.

'You mean you do like packing contraception for a night out?'

She laughed. 'No, I mean about the…you know.' She paused, wondering why she'd started this conversation. It wasn't going the way she'd expected. Too many years in the field where every topic was open for jokes and discussion. Living with the same people in such close proximity for such long periods of time stripped away social awkwardness. When she went bush, into remote areas, there'd often not even been the most basic opportunities for privacy. She felt so comfortable with Jock, she'd forgotten she was back where directness could be a shock, even when she was joking. 'I'm not really suggesting we get intimate…in that way.' She paused again and couldn't help teasing him. She met his gaze and grinned again, adding, 'Yet.'

'I wondered how long the demure Tilly would last.' He glanced at his watch. 'I believe it was seven seconds.'

'Too many years in the field. I've forgotten any social etiquette I ever had.'

'Your gran would be horrified.' He smiled at her, glancing down at her bare feet. She'd kicked her shoes off within seconds of getting into his car. 'But I suspect she already knows.'

She was about to comment when his mobile rang. He glanced at the screen display before saying, 'Can you hang on for a minute? I need to take this.'

CHAPTER SIX

JOCK recognised the number—it was his younger brother. He plugged in his earpiece before answering the call. This was one call he didn't want relayed through the speakers.

'Chris. How're things?'

He knew it was bad news before his brother had said more than two words. It was in his tone, the tone he used when he wanted something from Jock—which was pretty much the only time Jock heard from him.

He tried to keep his end of things neutral so Tilly wouldn't follow the gist of their conversation. That wasn't hard. Chris wasn't calling for advice or sympathy or to hear Jock's news, so he didn't want to hear a lot of words from his big brother. He was calling for money. Cash, preferably. A sizeable amount and as soon as possible. And why wouldn't he, when every time he'd come whining to his older sibling since Chris had been four and Jock seven Jock had fixed things for him, bailed him out, shored him up—more times than he cared to remember. Certainly more times than Chris had ever thanked him for.

Somehow it had become his role, his job, to take over responsibility for Chris and keep any extra stress from his parents.

'Mate, I'm just not in a position to help.' Hell, but those words sounded alien in his throat and even as he spoke them, he knew Chris wouldn't be taking no for an answer. He'd expect Jock to perform miracles and bail him out yet again, no matter what the inconvenience. 'Chris, I can't talk now, I'm driving. We'll discuss it later.'

He ended the call, shoved the phone back into its cradle, checked his mirrors and his blind spot and pulled back into the traffic, his mind still on the conversation. He was grateful that Tilly stayed silent, not asking who'd been on the phone, not pushing for information.

The worst part about it was that Chris was probably right. Jock would fold and do what had to be done to help his little brother out of strife. And he had to, didn't he? At the end of the day Jock had sold himself down the river when he'd agreed to be guarantor for Chris's latest business scheme. He was always giving him one last chance, giving him the benefit of the doubt, and he should have known better. But when did loyalty to family end and selfishness take over? When was it OK to turn your back on family, on *anyone* in need? And that's where he always got stuck, because he hadn't found the cut-off point yet, so he just kept on bailing Chris out.

Tilly stayed quiet until Jock pulled up at her house. He was tense again and from what she'd heard it sounded as if he had a brother who was in strife and was looking to Jock for assistance. And it sounded like Jock had almost choked on the words when he'd said he couldn't help. Which fitted with what she knew of him already: taking on responsibilities left, right and centre that weren't necessarily his. She had that helping streak, too, and it could be a killer sometimes, but she had a feeling Jock had skills in that domain that she was far from perfecting. Good thing, too, by the sound of it.

'So, are we on for tonight?' she ventured as she put her hand on the doorhandle and Jock still hadn't said anything about dinner.

He was tapping on the steering-wheel, looking even more harassed than she'd first seen him after his meeting that morning. 'I can't. My brother's arrived unexpectedly and I need to get home.' He stopped tapping and turned to her, an apologetic half-smile on his face as he said, 'I promise we'll find enough to do tomorrow to make the day stretch to dinner.'

'I do believe you're propositioning me, Dr Kelly,' she teased, eager to erase some of the worry lines on his brow and leave him on a happier note, hiding her disappointment that he hadn't confided in her.

This time his smile was more like the regular Jock-smile she'd already started to crave, and when he leant across and dropped a kiss on her forehead, the knot of tension that had risen in her stomach in the last ten minutes unfurled.

'I do believe you'd be the first to recognise it if I was, Dr Watson,' he said. He lowered his mouth and gently grazed his lips over hers, and the touch, though light, sent a tremor through her body. 'But if I don't leave now, your gran might get a shock if she was to look out the window in a few minutes.'

Tilly traced her index finger around the contours of his lips. '*Selamat tinggal,* then.'

'You speak Indonesian? Or are you—' his voice took on teasing tones '—one of those people who store up basic phrases so they can pretend?'

She pulled a face at him. '*Saudara orang yang sekali buruk.*'

'I gather that wasn't polite. And I gather you do speak Indonesian.'

'Those in the know call it Bahasa. And I said, "You're a very bad man."'

'So you're beautiful *and* clever.'

'Thank you.' She gave him a kiss full on the lips. 'That's what a girl needs to hear. Keep that up and…' she tapped her temple '…my headache might not need to make an appearance tomorrow after all.'

She opened the door, slipped out of the car and waved before closing it firmly, peering through the window to see him still laughing and shaking his head at her.

She ran up to the house and leapt up the stairs, turning at the front door to wave again and take one last look at the man over whom she was rapidly losing her well-practised self-control. Her attraction to him was growing in leaps and bounds in such a short time she was stunned by it. She was only here for three months so she'd made a conscious decision to make the most of that time. But in deciding that, she hadn't counted on being quite this keen on, well, pretty well everything about him, if she was honest with herself.

But she had a feeling, given how he sidestepped any attempt on her part to turn the conversation to more personal areas of his life, that if he felt she was getting too close, he'd back away. He was fantastic at listening and helping with the problems of others, she had firsthand proof of that in her own case, but he'd shown himself to be less than enthusiastic about confiding when it came to himself.

Fair enough, she told herself as she waited on the porch, watching as his car turned out of the driveway and out of view. In most circumstances, she'd let it go. She wasn't one to push, but if he was going to keep her at a distance to some degree, it could seriously lessen her prospects of him kissing her soundly every single day for the next eighty-two or so days. And she wanted the best odds on that she could get.

Five minutes after getting home, Jock was wishing he'd taken Tilly up on her offer. Chris hadn't even given him time to change before he was regaling him with his latest disaster. Jock would never turn his back on his siblings but for the first time he wished he was somewhere else. With Tilly, to be precise, he admitted to himself.

'Let me see if I've got this straight. You've bought a bigger boat but you haven't sold the other one.'

'Not yet.' There was a belligerence in his younger brother's tone that he didn't care for.

'And you've got repayments to make on both, plus payments

still owing from when you bought the business, none of which are being covered by your charter fees.'

'Wages and running costs account for a big portion of the outgoings and there isn't enough left to meet the repayments.'

'Why did you buy the new boat? What was wrong with leasing it?'

'I didn't think of it.'

Jock felt like punching something. His brother was thirty-five years old, running a business that he was clueless about and expecting Jock to bail him out. The trouble was that Jock had agreed to be Chris's guarantor so this debacle became his responsibility.

'If you could just lend me thirty grand to tide me over until I sell one boat, that's all I need.' Chris was asking for it as if he wanted Jock to pass him a glass of water. There was not so much as a whisper of embarrassment.

'The trouble is, Chris, I don't have that kind of money. Speak to the bank, explain the situation. Tell them they'll get their money if they can give you a bit more time.'

'I've already had two extensions on the repayments. They'll be calling you next.' Again, he spoke as if he were now relieved of all responsibility. 'I thought I'd speak to you first.'

So that was why he was there. Jock supposed that counted for something. Chris normally wouldn't even extend him that courtesy.

'I wish I could help but I don't see what I can do. Why don't you let me sleep on it? Come on, I'll grab you some sheets for the spare bed.' He felt like the parent of a child who was particularly hard work. But was that Chris's fault? He was the one who'd always been there. He'd encouraged Chris and Jules to rely on him from the time they'd both been little, when their parents hadn't seemed able to take the role that had been rightfully theirs. What right did Jock have to blame Chris for that now?

The sun was still low in the sky but already strong as Jock and Tilly made their way up another of the many inclines on the main track through the national park. Hugging the coast as it did, rising and falling through the scrub, it was a beautiful walk. Tilly looked out across the sea and felt a strong sense of calm descend on her.

Jock had been quiet so far. He seemed distracted and she could only assume it had something to do with his brother, but while he was silent she couldn't raise the topic without it sounding like she was prying.

So far neither of them had alluded to their conversation of the previous evening. She'd gone to bed quelling the thought that she might have frightened him off with her directness and flippancy, but despite his silence he seemed at ease with her and had found numerous ways of touching her that day. Taking her hand as they walked, placing a gentle touch on her arm as he pointed out something of interest to her, resting a hand on her upper back as they stopped and craned their necks to look for koalas hidden high in the grey-green foliage of the eucalypts. He didn't seem upset with her so she figured she'd just have to be patient.

'I always stop here,' he said, breaking the silence as he halted at a lookout point, and she felt her adrenalin surge in anticipation of his touch. He drew her against him and she relaxed into his side, feeling the hard contours of his body, muscled in all the right places but without any suggestion of the bulging, bodybuilder type she abhorred. She closed her eyes and tried to conjure up the image, just by resting against him, of what he'd looked like, shirt off, that first day on the beach.

It was quite an image and she sighed, then was distracted by the scent of him as she drew in her next breath. The morning scents of the scrub, the bush all around them, were blended with the scent of Jock, part sunblock, part *him*. One hundred percent male. One hundred percent *yummy*.

'Pardon?'

Tilly's eye snapped open and she realised Jock was watching

her intently, as he had when she'd come out of her dizzy spell at Cockatoo Gully.

'Are you OK?'

'Sure. Why?' She laughed but it sounded more like the giggle it actually was. She'd been sprung daydreaming by the object of the daydream.

'Are you sure? I was pointing out the view and it sounded like you said, "Yummy," but your eyes were closed.'

Oops. Seemed like she'd spoken her last thought out loud. 'Ah, yes.' The doubt on his face hadn't lessened. 'Really, I am.' He was still watching her closely, as if examining her for signs of fatigue or being unwell. 'Darn you, Jock Kelly.' She was laughing properly now. 'I'm only confessing this because I can see you're about to march me back to the car and tuck me under an invalid's rug.' She put her hands on her hips and looked him square in the eyes. 'If you must know, I wasn't thinking about the view. I was thinking about you.' She scrunched her face up a little, wrinkling her nose to express her mock distaste at her next comment. 'But don't go getting any ideas. You're not that hot.'

'But I *am* yummy.' He rubbed at an imaginary mark at the edge of his mouth, his expression suggesting he was giving this serious thought. 'At least *you*…' he reached and flicked her cap off before she realized what he was doing and caught it before it fell to the ground '…think I'm yummy.'

'And a touch arrogant.'

'Agreed, on both counts.' He pulled her cap firmly down over the top of her head then chucked her under the chin. 'If you were wondering, I am available to be lusted over until at least midnight tonight.' The grin stretched across his face might have seemed self-satisfied on anyone else, but on him it was just another weapon in his armoury of charm, charm she wasn't sure he really knew he had. Which was just as well, because in the hands of a professional it could be her absolute undoing.

'I never would've believed it. You *like* being lusted after.'

'Only by you.'

His voice had taken on huskier tones and it was an effort for her to speak rather than simply pull him down to her and kiss him hard on the mouth. But she'd promised herself last night that she'd go more slowly so she said, 'Glad to hear it.'

He didn't reply. He was looking over her shoulder at something that was distracting him. Tilly turned to follow his gaze. Coming up the incline towards them was an overweight, middle-aged man. He was jogging—at least, Tilly assumed that was what he was trying to do—but he was struggling. She could hear him gasping for air and he certainly didn't look as though he was used to physical exercise. He looked up and stopped as soon as he saw them. He leant forward, bending over his knees, resting his arms on his thighs, almost sagging in his tiredness.

Jock was by his side straight away. 'You OK?'

The man shook his head and between gasps said, 'Been an…accident. Wife's called…Emergency Services.' His words were staggered by great breaths for air. 'Thought I'd come show…where we are.'

'What's happened?'

'A kid's fallen down a cliff, 'bout one and a half k's.' He waved a hand in the direction from which he'd come. 'On the main track. Didn't see it happen, just heard a call for help.' His breathing was a little easier now but only a little.

'We're doctors. Can you tell us if the child seemed injured or just stuck?'

'Couldn't tell. It was hard to see. I didn't want to go too close to the edge.'

'I think you should wait here for the rescue team. I don't want them to have to treat you as well. We'll go back to meet your wife.'

'Her name's Loretta.'

He called out as Jock and Tilly darted off, sprinting as fast as the uneven bare earth of the path would allow them, watching for roots sticking up in odd places through the soil.

They dashed under the foliage, up and down inclines, some longer than others. They overtook other walkers, ran around other joggers, passing the point by which most walkers would've turned and headed back to the car park and heading into the quieter, less trammelled reaches of the park, though they were still on the main track hugging the coast. It felt further than one and a half kilometres, Tilly thought as she tried to keep up with Jock. After a particularly steep hill, they ran out into the full glare of the sun and Tilly groaned.

Jock didn't break stride but said, in an almost normal, pant-free voice, 'You OK? Stop if you need to and catch me up later.'

She shook her head to indicate she'd keep up. Talking was beyond her. She was, however, despite her competitiveness, about to bail and have a rest when she saw a middle-aged woman waving frantically at them. Knowing they'd arrived, Tilly couldn't help but slow down, letting Jock run on ahead.

Jock clearly already had all the information he needed from Loretta and was at the edge of the cliff, inspecting the site, when she reached the woman. She instructed Loretta to stay back from the edge and keep a lookout for Emergency Services while she joined Jock, trying to get her breath back under control.

'What have we got?' She stood back a metre behind him, waiting for him to let her know if it was safe for her to approach the cliff edge. He looked back at her and she could see his approval that she knew basic safety protocol.

He stepped back to join her. 'I can see him but I can't get down from here. The cliff edge has given way and it's almost a sheer drop after the first few metres, down onto rocks.'

'How far?'

'Seven or eight metres.'

A long way to fall if they weren't careful. She could feel her stomach twitching with apprehension. They needed a plan, then she'd be able to get her nerves under control. She looked around at their surroundings, mentally looking for a suitable place to attach abseiling equipment. 'We'll have to find an anchoring point for the ropes. Have an idea of what's around when the Country Fire Service get here.'

'I don't want to wait for the rescue team. That child is probably injured and more than likely in shock. I have to get down there.' Jock's tone was adamant.

'But you just said it's not possible.'

'Not from here, but I think I can make it down to the sea from a bit further along and then I'll climb back up. The ledge is only a metre or two above the water. Can you talk to the child from here, try to establish and maintain verbal contact?'

Her stomach was twitching again. She had a bad feeling about this. 'Don't you think we should wait for some back-up, some proper equipment at least?'

'I can do this, Tilly, and I think the child needs the company. I'd certainly like to know help was on the way if it was me. Can you try to talk to him?'

'OK.' She could do this for him. She lay on her stomach, squashing her nerves into submission. Being careful not to disturb any loose stones as she didn't want to send them tumbling over the edge, she forced herself to focus on the child and ignore thoughts of Jock slipping and sliding down the cliff face.

She could see the prostrate form of the child, unmoving, on the ledge below her. He looked to be about nine or ten years old. She called out, hoping for an answer, wanting to know if he was conscious, wanting to get his name. There was no response.

She called again, asking him to move an arm or hand if he could hear her. This time she was rewarded—he lifted his right forearm into the air.

'Stay where you are,' she yelled. She didn't want him moving the wrong way and falling further. 'What's your name?'

'Alex.' The reply was faint but at least he was coherent.

'There's a doctor on his way, he'll be coming up from the

water.' She looked to her right, searching for Jock, and saw him clambering over the rocks.

He stopped climbing and peered up at her, calling out, 'I can't see him from this angle. Can you guide me?'

'He's directly below me—you'll need to come further across.' Tilly waved him further to his right.

Jock nodded and continued working his way across the rocks, hugging the shoreline. Tilly heard voices behind her and swivelled her head in time to see the rescue team arrive. She left it to Loretta to explain the situation—she needed to stay in position in order to direct Jock. She turned her attention back to the events below her. Jock was almost in line with her now.

'OK,' she yelled. 'Start making your way up. He's conscious, his name's Alex.'

Tilly watched, waiting for Jock to reach the child. He was almost there and she was about to move away from the cliff edge when she saw him slip. She heard him swear as he landed hard on the rocks, his foot caught between two boulders.

Her heart was in her throat and her stomach was in knots. She watched him struggle to free his foot. That bad feeling was back.

CHAPTER SEVEN

'ARE you all right?'

Jock pulled his foot out and raised one hand in the air, making a circle with his thumb and forefinger, signalling he was OK. Tilly waited until he'd reached the ledge and started his examination before she carefully retreated.

The rescue team was busy attaching their abseiling equipment to a sturdy tree and she introduced herself before explaining the current situation.

'What's your plan?' she asked.

'One of us will go down, and then we'll need to determine the best way of retrieving everyone to the top of the cliff. We'll have to evacuate them from up here.'

As one of the team members was being harnessed up and attached to the ropes, a woman came running up to the group.

'Has a young boy passed by here? He's about this tall.' She held her hand up level with her shoulder. 'He has brown hair and is wearing a red T-shirt.'

'Is his name Alex?' Tilly asked the question, capturing the woman's attention.

'Yes. Have you seen him?'

Tilly nodded.

'Which way did he go? He was throwing a ball and ran ahead and I lost him. He's always doing that.'

The woman's head was turning left and right, searching for her son. Tilly led her away from the rescue group, positioning herself between the woman and the cliff edge. She didn't want her running to the edge and causing another accident.

'Can you tell me your name?'

'Ros.'

'OK, Ros, I need you to listen to me.' Tilly put her hand on Ros's arm, ready to restrain her if necessary. 'There's been an accident. Alex is going to be OK—there's a doctor with him.'

'Where is he? Is he hurt? What happened?'

The woman was understandably agitated and Tilly tried to deliver the information in the best order so as not to distress her any further. 'I'm not exactly sure what happened. It seems he ducked under the guard rail and the edge of the cliff was unstable and gave way. He slipped but he landed on a ledge, which broke his fall.'

'I want to see him. Where is he?'

'The CFS is here, they'll be lifting him back up. You need to stay back from the edge. It's not stable and any further collapse could put Alex or someone else at risk. We can get an update from the emergency services team.'

Tilly hoped they'd had time to work out the state of things while she'd waylaid Alex's mother. She steered the woman back to the team and noted that one member had abseiled over the edge.

'Guys, this is Ros—she's Alex's mum. How is he?'

'Doc Kelly says he's OK. One of our guys is down there, too, we've got radio contact now. Alex has a broken leg and possibly a fractured pelvis, plus a few scratches and bruises but it could have been a lot worse. By the sound of it, he was pretty lucky. We're bringing him up now.'

Once Ros heard her son was going to be OK, her emotions got the better of her and she burst into tears. One of the CFS crew handed Tilly a blanket and she wrapped it around Alex's mother and tried to calm her down so she wouldn't upset her son.

'He's going to be all right. Everything's going to be fine.'

Tilly wasn't even sure her words were sinking in. The woman was shaking and crying and repeating, 'my baby, my baby,' over and over again. But Tilly kept on, hoping some of what she said would get through.

Alex and a CFS officer appeared, strapped together, with Alex immobilised on a spinal board. His mother's tears ceased the moment she saw him and she rushed to his side. Tilly let her go. The CFS could take over and she wanted to wait for Jock.

A second rope with a harness attached had been lowered down to him. She saw the rope move as Jock tugged on it, making sure it was firmly anchored, and heard him acknowledge everything was set to go. The CFS team started pulling him up the cliff. Tilly's heart was in her mouth as she waited for him to come into view. She knew how Alex's mother must have felt, unable to do anything except wait and hope, and Jock wasn't even hurt.

She saw him search the crowd when he reached the top of the cliff, his gaze meeting hers and resting there. She was by his side in an instant, wrapping her arms around him before he was un-harnessed.

'Hey, if you let me get out of these ropes, I can hug you properly.'

Tilly made a noise that was half laugh, half cry. 'Sorry. When I saw you slip I realised again how dangerous it was down there. I'm just so pleased to see you in one piece.' She stepped back as Jock quickly divested himself of the harness.

'I'm fine, but you look a bit shaky.'

Her legs felt wobbly and she knew it was from the aftermath of the adrenalin rushing through her body. Jock took a step towards her, wrapping her in his arms, supporting her.

'There's barely a scratch on me but I think I've had enough exercise for one day. How about the minute Alex is airlifted out of here, we head home?'

'Sounds good,' she said, although she was quite content to remain in his arms for the rest of the day. She made no move to

leave his embrace until he had to let her go in order to undo his
harness and check on Alex once more. Tilly heard the unmistak-
able sound of a helicopter approaching and watched it land a few
hundred metres from them, CFS officers keeping the area clear.
Alex and his mum were secured on board for the flight to
Brisbane and only once the chopper had taken off did Tilly and
Jock make their way out of the park.

As Jock turned into Tilly's driveway to collect her for dinner, a
searing anticipation at the night ahead spread through him.

He'd been lost in his thoughts earlier in the day, trying to
devise a solution to the predicament he found himself in thanks
to Chris. Somehow Tilly had managed to get him to put those
thoughts aside. He hadn't solved the dilemma yet and he'd surprised himself by keeping this date with Tilly. His siblings would
normally have first priority. Although, to be honest, he had
wavered a bit until Julianne had stepped in, threatening to frog-
march him to the car.

Now, as Tilly met him at the door, he said a silent thank you
to his sister. Tilly looked delicious.

She swung her long legs into the car and waited for him to shut
her door. He headed around to his side, continuing to mull things
over as he settled himself. What was it about her that pushed
thoughts of all the out-of-control aspects of his usually ordered
life into the background? Whatever it was, he wanted more of it.
More than he'd bargained for when she'd first appeared in his life,
sopping wet, trying in vain to haul a deadweight youth from the
water onto a jet-ski, her long legs rising above him, bare but for
the briefest of shorts as he'd swum up to the water-craft, her hair
pulled back into a dripping mess of a ponytail.

She was a puzzle, this Tilly Watson. Independent, yet soft as
butter, full of love for her grandparents yet able to spend years
away from them at a time. She was kind and gentle, yet held
something of herself back. Tilly could be as serious as anything

about some things but full of a teasing, playful spirit about others. And while perhaps not classically beautiful, she was arresting all the same and, for all her charm and high-achieving background, without an ounce, as far as he could see, of vanity.

He'd never met a woman who could get ready in such a short time. And without a handbag to boot.

Which reminded him. He started the car and reversed out of the driveway, giving her another appreciative glance for good measure and noting a few details he'd previously missed. 'Where do you keep all your secret women's things in that outfit? You don't have a handbag.' He turned into the main road and headed back into town.

'Quite the observant doctor.' She paused. 'Why, did you think you could shove all your bits and pieces in my bag?'

'Now you mention it, these keys and my mobile do get quite heavy. Not to mention my lip balm, my hand-cream…'

'You don't—'

He laughed. 'No, I don't. Just wanted to challenge your perception of me as a strait-laced doctor.'

'And you want me to see you as a metrosexual instead?'

'Is that what it's called?'

'Yes, but unless you've got facial and body-care products in here…' She lifted the lid of the console between the seats then pressed open the glove box, rummaging through the contents. 'You don't, so you don't qualify.' She patted him on the leg and he was glad it was dark in the car because his reaction was instant and unsubtle.

Should she or shouldn't she? She'd been grappling with that question since the trip to Brisbane yesterday. Fishing for information wasn't her style but she was increasingly intrigued about Jock. Her dreams were filled with images of kissing him—even the scent of him seemed to pervade her nights. As she closed her eyes before sleep, his face was the last vision that swam in her mind, and on waking, headache or no headache, she bounded out of bed if she knew she'd see him that day. It was natural to want to dig a little deeper, find out more about what made the man tick. Sure it was.

'Sorry to disappoint you, but you don't make the grade,' she said. 'But you do seem to be in touch with your feminine side, so you show some promise.' The horrified look he threw her way had her grinning and she ignored the flutter of nervousness at the fact that she was about to open herself to a giant rebuff. 'Take your family, for instance. You seem very close.' She decided to keep the teasing angle going. That way, if he really was averse to letting her in, they could both pretend she hadn't been serious about her quest for information. 'Meaningful chats with your brother, still living with your sister at the ripe old age of…'

'Thirty-eight.' So there was the answer to that question. 'And we don't live together. Jules lives in the cottage, she just—'

'Cooks all your meals,' she finished for him, and he laughed.

They were in Noosa now and Jock entered a car park just behind the main street. 'How did you find that out?'

Tilly beat him out of the car as soon as he'd parked and he shot her a look that said if she'd waited, he'd have helped her out. She just laughed and got back to the conversation as they headed out of the car park and into the main street. She didn't know where he'd booked and she didn't care. It was enough just to be with him—location was of little importance.

'I bumped into Jules on the beach on Thursday evening, and we got talking.'

'Do I want to hear this?'

'No need to be nervous.' Tilly laughed. 'She didn't dish too much dirt. But she told me no matter how hard she tries to give you the hint that you're cramping her style, if she's cooking, you appear in her kitchen the minute the food is ready. Never before.' She paused as she debated the etiquette of slipping her hand in his, but decided against it for now. She was being forward enough with her quizzing. 'She suspects you hang about on the veranda until you know it's ready then come in, so you don't have to chop anything.'

'Let me guess. I fail as a metrosexual on that count, too.'

'Definitely. You'd have to be able to sauté and blanch and whisk your way around the kitchen.' She paused. 'Unless you can cook but you just like spending time with your baby sister.' For some reason, he looked at her a little blankly at that, but said nothing so she went on. 'So what is it with you and your siblings? I never got that experience so I'm always interested about what it's like to be close to your family.' She hoped he'd buy that excuse for her prying. The truth was, she'd never been remotely interested in what it was like to have brothers or sisters.

They'd reached the end of Hastings Street just before it curved and headed up into the national park and she guessed where they were having dinner. It was the very restaurant she'd pick for a romantic date, complete with views out to the ocean across moonlit sand and soft lighting inside, added to incredible food and discreet service. They were seated, with menus presented and still water poured into oversized glasses, before he answered her. If he didn't want to talk about his family he'd had the perfect opportunity to change topics but he didn't.

'I'm closest to Jules. As for my brother...' Jock paused and ran his fingers through his hair, ruffling it and looking very sexy as a result. 'I've taken care of Chris since he was four and I was seven. And of Jules, too, I guess, since she was six or so.' His eyes sparkled from seriousness to laughter. 'Except for cooking.'

They both laughed and looked up as the waiter came to pour their wine and tell them about the specials. Tilly paid no attention to what she was ordering—anything would be amazing here anyway and her mind was busy with the information Jock had given her—and went straight back to the conversation the moment the waiter left. She neither remembered nor cared what she'd ordered. Jock seemed to be opening up and the only goal she had in mind was to make the most of the opportunity to get to know him more.

'What happened when you were seven? You said you've been looking out for Chris since then.'

'I had another sister, five years younger than me. Laura,' he said, and the penny dropped. There had been another sister younger than Jules. 'When she was two, she was diagnosed with leukaemia and spent most of the next eighteen months in hospital. She died just before my ninth birthday so I remember it pretty well.' From his tone she knew he was understating just how searing his memories were of that time.

'How awful. I'm really sorry, Jock.' She sipped at her drink, not sure whether to feel bad at having pushed for this insight into the man opposite her or glad that she'd achieved her goal of breaking through some of his barriers. That experience, drawn-out as it was, would have had a profound effect on a child of that age. 'So the role of responsible oldest brother took on a whole new meaning for you during that time.'

The look on his face said she'd presented him with the very heart of the impact that time had had on him.

'Basically, yes. Mum and Dad spent most of their time in hospital with Laura and we stayed with relatives. There were no facilities for families with children other than the sick child to spend time together during treatment.'

'Hence the unit,' breathed Tilly, another piece of the puzzle falling into place.

'I guess that's right.' He sipped at his wine then swirled the liquid, watching the colours play against the glass. 'I hadn't really thought of it that way, but my experience as a child must have been what made me aware of the need for such a facility.' He shook his head and placed his glass back on the table but kept his hand on the stem, twirling it, not looking at Tilly, and she guessed his mind was busy in the past.

She stayed silent, giving him the time he needed to continue. 'The upshot was that our parents weren't overly available for us, as you can imagine. Even when Laura died, their grief far exceeded ours and Mum especially was never the same after that. Chris was too young to understand anything much and Jules and I, although older, didn't have very clear memories of Laura by the time she died. We'd seen her now and again in hospital but she'd been out of our everyday lives for so long it didn't really come as much of a shock or a sense of loss when she died. If anything, we were happy to move back home with Mum and Dad except that, like I've said, it was never the same again. It's more the effect it had on our lives that had the greatest impact rather than the loss of a sister.' His laugh was dry, out of place with his words. 'I sound like an ogre. My little sister died and here I am whingeing about how I was hard done by.'

Tilly's heart went out to him. 'You're perfectly entitled to feel as you do. It's not saying you don't care about Laura to want your own losses acknowledged. It's OK.'

He met her eyes at that, for the first time since he'd started talking about Laura, and the relief she saw there, the gratitude that someone understood and hadn't judged him, was overwhelming. Instinctively, she knew the shutters would come down in a moment if she didn't tread very carefully. Here was a grief still raw, untouched, after thirty years. He'd assumed the role of parent to his younger siblings but had never had his own loss acknowledged. The loss of his right to be a child to be parented without assuming the mantle of parenting himself. She tried to put it into words, to help steer him through the grief he'd shelved so many years before. She just hoped she hadn't read it all wrong or he'd shut her out immediately. She steeled herself and took a risk that her interpretation was right.

'You became a parent figure when you were just a little boy,' she said, her voice soft. 'You have a right to be angry about that, you have a right to be sad about what you lost. You lost a sister but in a real sense it sounds as though you also lost your boyhood.'

He was still toying with his glass, twirling it between his fingers. He was silent, but he didn't correct or reject what she was saying. In her limited experience, that meant she was at least close to the mark.

'And since then you've kept taking care of Chris and Jules, shouldering the responsibility your parents didn't resume.'

She guessed some more, too, but she didn't know him well enough to question him along those lines. How could she indirectly ask whether he was still taking on too much responsibility? Besides, it was just a hunch after that phone call, and it would hardly be acceptable to respond to Jock's revelations with what would sound like a criticism of his role in his brother's life. Plus, it was clear from the slightly stilted way in which he'd told her the story that it did count as a revelation and that it had been a long time, if ever, since he'd put the tale into words. He'd had the look of someone being mentally in another world as he'd spoken, and not once had he looked at her.

But he looked at her now, and she guessed the rueful grin on his face was an attempt to mask his feelings about being confronted with the loss he'd denied to himself for so long. 'That's about the size of it. Old habits die hard. It's not so bad with Jules but with Chris...' He paused. 'With Chris, I think I may be responsible for ensuring he's never grown up.'

Tilly flicked her eyes over his upper body and he watched her, a bemused expression on his face. 'You're well built across the shoulders, Jock, but it's still a lot of responsibility you're hoisting on them.' It was ridiculous for him to be blaming himself for his brother's shortcomings. 'If Chris is a few years younger than you, he's all grown up now.'

'I'm not saying he hasn't contributed, but I've always dug him out of trouble so he assumes I always will. I'll always help Jules out, too, but she's been blessed with some basic common sense so she doesn't get herself into the same scrapes.'

It hadn't escaped her notice that he'd ignored the question of what he might have lost when his sister had died. He'd shifted the conversation straight back to his siblings' experience, whether or not he realised it. There was only so much she could push, so she followed his lead—at least he was still opening up to her.

'Where are your parents now?'

'In New Zealand. Dad's side of the family is there. They moved back about fifteen years ago.'

Leaving Jock to be the head of the family in Australia, she guessed. 'Do you mind if I ask what Chris has done?'

He shrugged and she knew before he spoke she was about to receive the edited version. 'Financial trouble. I agreed to be the guarantor for him on a business he wanted to start up. I was hoping he'd finally make a go of something but it seems as though this scheme has gone the way of all his others.'

'What sort of business?'

'A fishing charter out of Townsville. He was working for the company at the time. He'd been with them nearly a year, which for Chris was long-term employment. His boss wanted to sell out and retire and Chris convinced me he'd be able to make a go of it. Unfortunately, being a boss and being an employee are two different things.'

'What went wrong?'

Jock did the sexy hair ruffle thing again, apparently oblivious to its effect on Tilly, making her struggle to concentrate on his answer. 'It seems as though my little brother has overextended himself. I was the guarantor for his original loan but he's taken out another loan, which he can't meet the repayments for. As far as I can make out, the bank is about to call in both loans.'

'What will you do?'

'I'm not sure yet. Until I can speak to the bank, I'm in the dark. As usual, Chris was fairly sketchy with the details.'

'And you think it'll be bad news.'

'It's the only kind I get from Chris.' His expression was grim.

'Will you help him?'

He laughed. 'Despite all the ranting and railing I'll get from Jules, yes, if I can, I probably will. As guarantor I probably won't have a choice. I keep saying that it's the last time, but—'

'You can't turn your back on family,' she finished off.

He nodded. 'Jules says I'm making it worse for him and until he's left to flounder by himself he'll never learn. Funny thing is, I know she's right, but how do I tell Chris?'

She watched as a mix of emotions played across his face before his expression settled and he met her gaze. 'Enough about that. It's not something we can fix tonight so let's put away the violins. I want to hear more about you.'

'Don't you think I warrant violins?'

'Spoilt little rich girl like you, kissing the publican's son in a cupboard?' She pulled a face at him and he added, 'I doubt it.'

'I wasn't rich. Gran was the one who inherited Dalgerie station, not me. I was never spoilt.' She ticked her protests off on her fingers. 'And technically it wasn't a cupboard. And on top of that, my parents *did* die when I was a baby so don't I get the teensiest little violin playing? I might not remember it, but it's a fact that usually warrants lots of sighing and regrets from people.'

'Which you hate.'

She was surprised at that. How did he know that about her? 'Actually, yes, I do. I don't feel sorry for myself. I can't miss what I didn't know.'

'What happened to your parents?' He paused. 'If you don't mind me asking.'

'I don't mind. I owe you a few answers.' Once again he'd turned the conversation away from himself. 'My parents were only nineteen when I was born. By all accounts they weren't ready for the responsibility of raising a child and left it to my mum's parents. I gather they'd rather indulged my mother until she had me, then they expected her to act responsibly. Mum ran off after an argument with my grandparents and left me behind, which apparently wasn't unusual, but that particular night she didn't come back. My parents' car collided with a road train and they were killed.'

'And your grandparents brought you up.' Tilly nodded. 'Until you were sent to boarding school. It sounds a lonely sort of a childhood.'

She shook her head. 'It wasn't. I just learned to be self-sufficient. Besides, plenty of the station workers had kids and I played with them. Some were like family.'

'I can't imagine growing up without my siblings around me, as much as they drive me wild from time to time. And I don't think I could send my children away to boarding school.'

'Why not?'

'I promised myself I'll always be there for my kids, no matter what.'

'I can understand why you might feel like that, but that's a pretty big promise. And sending them to boarding school doesn't mean you're not there for them—it usually means you're giving them the best education available. The options are limited when you live on the land.'

Jock shrugged. 'I like to think that no one could do a better job of raising my children than me.'

She hid a smile. His answer fitted exactly with what she already knew about him, stepping into the role of responsible adult, taking on more than he necessarily needed to. At least now she had a better idea of the family background that had helped make him that way.

'You haven't had enough of parenting after taking care of Chris and Jules for so long?'

'Not at all. I'm looking forward to doing it with my own children. I can only improve.' He was smiling but was he asking for reassurance?

'I'm sure you'll be great, but children need more than just their primary care-givers, parents or otherwise, especially as they get older. I suspect my grandparents tried to be all things to my mother and that she rebelled against that, but at the same time she knew they'd bail her out if she ran into problems. I gather she never learned to be independent and that's not good. At some point children have to learn to stand on their own two feet.'

'Like you.'

Tilly nodded. 'And you, too, by the sound of things.'

'What about your father's family? Could you have lived with them to go to school?'

'He was an only child, too, and I never saw his parents. Apparently they weren't interested in me.' Tilly shrugged. 'They're dead now anyway. Besides, I'm glad I went away to school. It helped shape me into what I am today.'

'You'll feel differently when you have your own children.'

'I'm not having any. My work's all I need.'

He'd forgotten about that, she'd mentioned it before. Was it really just because of her dedication to work or had her upbringing made her reluctant to have a family of her own? He found himself curious about it but unwilling to question her on this topic now. They'd covered enough ground for one evening.

'Have lunch with Jules and me tomorrow. Come over to my place. You'll probably meet Chris, too. Get a taste of what life with siblings is all about.'

She laughed. 'Lunch would be lovely but it won't change anything. Like I said before, you can't miss what you've never known.'

'The philosophical side to Jungle Tilly.'

'Is that really how you think of me? Jungle Tilly? You sound like my grandmother.'

He watched her for a moment, a smile touching the corners of his mouth. 'I think of you in a lot of ways.' His gaze trailed down to her mouth and lingered there. 'But most of all I think of you as kissable. I've never thought of pubs as fondly as I do now.'

She laughed. It was the most direct reference either of them had made tonight to their kiss at Cockatoo Gully. Thoughts of family histories went spinning out of her mind as every bit of her focused on the physical sensations racing through her body. The merest allusion to 'the kiss' and she was melting. She struggled to think of a reply but all she could do was grin back at him and wrap one ankle tightly around the chair leg to stop herself from climbing onto his lap there and then.

'How's your head tonight? Any trace of a headache?' he asked, throwing her for a minute until she remembered her parting tease last night.

'Not a bit. And if I receive another of those kisses you've mentioned, I think I might never have another one. I suspect they're highly medicinal.'

'That…' he leaned over the table and with a slow, light touch brushed his thumb across her lips, lingering at the corner as her mouth curved into a smile '…can be arranged.' The darkening of his slate-coloured eyes underlined his promise and Tilly found herself immediately restless, eager now for dinner to be over. The only thing she needed to complete her night was another of Jock's delectable kisses.

He'd been as good as his word and the kisses they'd shared as they'd walked along the moonlit beach after dinner had made sleep impossible. She'd tossed and turned most of the night, thoughts of Jock interrupting her sleep. She couldn't remember ever being so attracted to someone. The attraction had been instantaneous and hadn't lessened as she'd learned more about him.

She'd just been drifting off when a thought had had her eyes flying open, wide awake. If they kept this up, if she had her way and was kissed on a daily basis by him, how was she going to leave it all behind and return to Indonesia?

She'd never had trouble saying goodbye before. Everything in life was transitory, life itself was fleeting and nothing stayed the same. That had always been perfect by her. For the first time she was struck by anxiety about things changing.

And that was only after a couple of kisses.

What happened if their relationship progressed to a more intimate level? What happened once she'd got used to him being part of her daily life? How did she just walk away then?

Chewing on her fingernails, a long-ago habit she'd thought long since gone, she sat up in bed, debating her options. When she'd decided she'd wanted oodles of kisses, she'd thought she'd been in control, making a simple choice, but that choice was rapidly taking on a life of its own.

Just like her libido. She couldn't get enough of him after this short time. How on earth was she going to feel after another two-plus months?

She'd fought hard to prove to herself and her grandparents that she could not only thrive on her own but do it in circumstances that would have had most people running scared. Regardless of the lack of an emotional connection with her gran, she knew Flo respected her drive and courage in making her own way in the world, the importance of which had been drilled into Tilly from her earliest days. Tilly had never fallen short of Flo's high standards in that regard, unlike her poor mum who'd given them nothing but disappointment.

She'd have to tread warily to ensure she didn't sacrifice her independence.

She finally gave up any pretence of sleep, opting instead for an early morning trip to the hillside markets of Eumundi. She avoided the craft stores for the moment, heading instead for the fresh produce area to pick up ingredients for the salad she'd promised to take to Jock's for lunch. Trays of local mangoes and punnets of strawberries, so red they looked as if they'd been painted, lined the trestle tables. Tilly couldn't resist the smell of the ripe mangoes and selected half a dozen, two for the salad and the rest to eat at home. She chose strawberries and baby spinach leaves, planning on making a green salad with a twist before she wandered back to the arts and crafts, ostensibly to browse and watch the crowds, but her mind was really running on repeat loop through a mantra—independence, independence, independence.

* * *

An hour into lunch and Tilly's mantra was receiving no end of help from Jock's brother, Chris, the perfect antidote to any thoughts of sacrificing independence for settling down with a family.

She'd been aware that she'd already formed an opinion of Chris and had forced herself to come to lunch prepared to be proved wrong, but Chris wasn't making it easy.

While he physically resembled Jock, although stockier, their characters were poles apart. She hadn't needed many minutes before her first impressions were confirmed: Chris was as self-absorbed as Jock was generous, as flighty as Jock was stable. It was obvious why Chris needed Jock, but what did Jock get from the relationship except for a bucketload of angst? Chris was trouble with a capital T.

Even lunch was a testament to Chris's selfishness. Jock had barbecued fillets of red emperor, one of the best of the local fish, served accompanied by Julianne's shoestring chips and Tilly's salad. If Chris had contributed anything towards lunch, Tilly couldn't see it and nothing was mentioned. She felt petty but she was really beginning to wonder why Jock was so supportive of his brother. And how Chris could live with himself when all he did was take, take, take.

'You live next door, do you, Tilly?' That was the first time in an hour Chris had made any attempt to find out anything about her, despite her generous attention to his life.

'My grandmother does. I'm just visiting.' She could hear the terseness in her voice. She didn't want to sound like that but everything about Chris irritated her. Selfish and smug and, worst of all, no apparent justification for his arrogance.

'From where?'

'Indonesia.'

There was a pause and Tilly could almost see the wheels turning. 'What's the demand for fishing charters up your way?'

Tilly was very tempted to ask where Chris was planning on

getting the money for that little investment but thought better of it as it really wasn't her concern.

'None where I work. It's not a tourist destination and the local people don't have the time or money to spend on expensive charters. They're too busy trying to survive.'

'Are you on the coast? Surely even the locals eat fish.'

'Of course. But they fish for a living or to feed their families, not for sport.' If Chris picked up her tone, he ignored it.

'What about the tourist destinations, then?'

'I don't visit there but what from I've heard they're pretty well catered for.' She was getting the distinct impression Chris hadn't learnt much from his recent business failure. Was he seriously thinking about moving to Indonesia? On such a spur-of-the-moment thought and the strength of her information? If this was how all his schemes began, she could understand why his success rate was so abysmal. And why didn't Jock and Jules say something? She waited, giving them an opportunity. Maybe they were as amazed as she was.

She looked at Jock, who was looking a bit stunned, then Jules, who was looking at Jock. Was she waiting for him to speak first? Did his siblings both always look to him before making decisions?

Jock finally seemed to recover his power of speech.

'Mate, there are a few problems to sort out here first, before you go looking for more trouble.'

'This might be just the opportunity I'm looking for.' Chris's voice was confident. Deluded was the word that sprang to Tilly's mind.

'That's what you said about the Townsville charter, if my memory serves me correctly,' Jock replied.

Chris dismissed him with a wave of his hand. 'All those wealthy tourists and my own slice of paradise. Indonesia is an untapped gold mine. What do you reckon, Tilly?'

Since he was asking for her opinion, she decided to let him have it. With both barrels.

'Most people would consider Townsville and the rest of Far North Queensland to be as close to paradise as they could expect to find. And, as I said, I don't know much about the tourist industry or business opportunities in Indonesia, but I would imagine it's quite difficult for a foreigner to set up a business—'

Chris interrupted, an unattractive smirk on his face. 'That's easily solved. I'd just attract an Indonesian business associate.'

Female ones, she supposed. His blond highlights were definitely fake. She'd bet money he had tips done to match the sun-bronzed surfie image tourists had of Australians, a blatant attempt to woo the ladies rather than focusing any marketing on his actual target market: men. She just knew it. 'I'd think any investor would want to know your business history before they threw their money in…' She left the rest of her sentence unspoken. Everyone present knew Chris wouldn't pass that inspection.

Chris snorted but said nothing and looks were flying every which way across the table, the tension tangible as silence fell. It was clear Jock wasn't going to put Chris in his place and, from the challenge in the look Chris was giving Jock, she knew suddenly that if anyone was going to be put in their place, it was her. Fine, she thought, the fight rising in her. Seeing a less perfect side to Jock would only serve to help her maintain her independence, even if it didn't overly dampen her physical attraction to him.

Then Chris rolled his eyes in her direction. And turned his back on her, making a big show of helping himself to more salad. But she knew it was a rebuff.

And Tilly couldn't control her response.

'You think it's funny? Expecting people to let you waste their money and then putting your hand out for more?' She couldn't believe his cheek.

'I assume you're referring to me there.' Jock's voice was quiet but steely. 'But that's where you've got it wrong. Family is all about people who love you no matter what and can be depended on.'

She'd wanted to see a less perfect side to Jock, she knew she'd even been angling to provoke him, but the reality shocked her. Not that he'd be able to see that. In times of stress her fight reaction had always been stronger than the urge to flee. 'Love isn't about bailing the same people out from the same mistakes over and over. Children maybe, not adults.'

'Perhaps that's the case for you, but maybe your family is the unusual one,' said Jock as Chris leant back in his chair, stuffing his mouth with forkful after forkful of salad—*her* salad—clearly enjoying the unfolding scene.

'Besides…' Jock seemed to be trying to force some lightness into his tone. 'If you ever needed help, I'm sure Flo would be there for you.'

Tilly wasn't so sure. She'd been raised to be independent and she doubted her pride would ever let her ask for help. The same pride that wouldn't let her back down now. 'I'd never expect her to fix my mistakes. Is that what you're saying? That you'd support Chris in his next venture, despite what's happened?'

'If I could, yes. I'd never refuse Jules or Chris any help I was able to give. But I'm not in a position to help him financially again right at this moment, we all know that.'

She shrugged, horrified at the scene she'd helped create, stirred up by Chris, yes, but she'd sailed in there, too, boots and all, and there was no way she could see to backtrack from her part without Chris thinking he'd won. 'I guess that's your decision to make.'

Chris was the only one who didn't seem to be squirming with discomfort. He was grinning at Tilly from the other side of the table, looking like the cat who'd got the canary. She glared back at him. 'And you're happy to keep asking for more? At your age?' How could he live with himself?

'As he said, we're family.' He narrowed his eyes at her, unseen by Jock who was sitting beside him, his voice dripping with fake sweetness. 'Blood is thicker than water.'

CHAPTER EIGHT

TILLY waited for Jock to dispute Chris's words. But there was nothing but silence around the table. She couldn't bear to think she'd misread Jock so completely.

'If you'll excuse me, I need to get home.' She folded her napkin, placing it carefully beside her plate, calm and controlled, before pushing her chair back from the table. 'Thank you for lunch.' Her upbringing didn't allow her to storm from the table.

Even though she thought they were misguided, they were a family and their business was just that. Their business. She shouldn't have entered the fray. Chris just seemed to know exactly which buttons to push to get a rise out of her. And, boy, had she risen. She needed some space before she said something, or rather anything else, she might regret.

Jock and Jules both stood as she left the table. Chris stayed slouched in his chair, his smirk back in place. How she'd love to wipe it from his face. 'Don't get up. I'll see myself out,' she said, and left the back veranda where they'd been seated.

As she walked around the side of the house, she realised Jock was behind her. She slowed her steps so he could catch up and hopefully explain why he couldn't let go of being the big brother.

She stopped and turned around, but it was Jules who had followed her out, a tentative smile in place, like she was unsure of her reception.

'Don't be angry with Jock, Tilly.' Jules reached out a hand and touched Tilly on the arm. When Tilly nodded to show she was listening, she went on. 'Between you and Chris, he was sandwiched in an impossible place, between the two extremes of dependence and independence. No one's ever challenged him before about how he handles Chris, except me. It took him by surprise and so, of course, old habits took over and he defended Chris. It's what he's been doing since he was a little boy.' She smiled but still looked tense and a fresh wave of guilt swept through Tilly. She'd had no right to ruin the lunch and stress Jules, who'd been nothing but kind and friendly from the first moment they'd met.

'I owe you an apology. I ruined your lunch and I shouldn't have said what I did.' Tilly paused. Apologies could only cover so much ground. 'Even if it was true.'

Jules laughed and Tilly knew she'd found a friend. And probably lost Jock. Quite a feat for an hour-long lunch.

'Chris is appalling, and I say that as a loving sister. He's never grown up and he needs a great big dose of reality. I'm hoping this time will be it.'

Tilly nodded. 'Good luck.'

The dryness of her tone made her thoughts on the chances clearer than she'd intended. Jules screwed her face up with concern and sighed. 'I don't like the odds either.'

She looked over her shoulder as Chris called her name. 'I'm being summoned. I'm no match for my brothers, one so loving he'd smother me with kindness if I let him and the other so selfish he'd sell the clothes from my back if he needed the money.' She giggled like it was something she could cope with and Tilly's laugh in response was spontaneous. 'I'll see you again? Don't let today put you off me. I've only been back here living on Jock's property for a few months and I could do with a friend.' She held out her arms and Tilly stepped into her hug, stooping a little as Jules was much shorter. Then Jules waved and headed back the way she'd come, leaving Tilly to walk home alone, reflecting with not a little discomfort on the afternoon's events.

Jules had surpassed herself with her good breeding. Chris had been everything Tilly had expected. And Jock?

She didn't know what to think about Jock.

His generous nature was one of the many things she found attractive but she'd seen another side to him today and, despite knowing she'd been as much to blame as Chris for their altercation, it had been something she hadn't expected. He'd sided with his younger brother, without any attempt to put him in his place, and had let her take all the responsibility.

Twelve hours ago, after dinner, when his arms had been around her and he'd been kissing her as if she were the only other person under the sun, she'd have bet everything on him taking her side when goaded by his oaf of a brother.

So it looked like Chris had been right about one thing. Maybe blood really was thicker than water, in which case she hadn't needed to recite her mantra of independence after all. Jock Kelly wasn't the man she'd thought he was and her freedom had never been in danger.

Jock pressed the redial button on his desk phone for the third time that half-hour and listened with increasing irritation to his brother's voicemail message. Chris had headed back to Townsville the previous day after the run-in with Tilly and wasn't returning any of his calls. Jock had lost count of the messages he'd left since he'd spoken with SunCoast Bank. He slammed the handset back into its cradle, not bothering to leave another message.

He couldn't believe Chris was avoiding him. Especially not when he'd agreed to do what he could do help him out— again—and had even sided with him against Tilly. He was seriously beginning to question why he'd done that. Chris's behaviour now certainly didn't imply that he appreciated the support. Jules was furious with both of her brothers and Jock could see her point of view.

He put his head into his hands. He'd had nothing but bad news that day and his temper was stretched. The news from the bank wasn't quite what he'd expected.

It was worse.

Chris's plant and equipment were not going to raise the required funds, which meant the bank was calling in the loans. Jock had no spare cash, only the collateral. And the collateral was his property. His home. And at present Jules's home, too.

Jock massaged his temples—increasingly tight since Friday's meeting with the health minister—they were now beginning to burn. His headache turned his mind again to Tilly.

He hadn't realised just how different their views were. She was so able to stand on her own two feet, whereas he defined himself with reference to his siblings. He really didn't have the energy to figure out what he was going to do about her right now, much as he knew he had to—no, much as he knew he *wanted* to—whatever the resolution.

That problem would have to wait. His mind turned back to the most pressing issue. And the way things were going, it would be overtaken by something even more depressing within the hour.

Glancing at his watch, he picked up the phone again. No point putting off the inevitable. Jules had to be told he'd lost the house and the property. Or, rather, their little brother had. It was something he'd rather not do over the phone but since he'd given the real estate agent permission to go over the property before he even arrived home that evening, there was no way around it.

She answered on the seventh ring. 'Jules, Jock here. How's your day so far?'

Jules told him a bit about her morning, her voice a little cool since yesterday's lunch, but at least she was talking to him. For now, anyway. Perhaps not when he'd given her the news. 'But you haven't rung to hear about that,' she was saying, 'so what's up?'

'Bad news. You know I put the property up as collateral for Chris's business?'

'Tell me it's not that bad.' Sympathy replaced the coolness in Jules's tone. She'd worked it out immediately, just as he'd hoped she would. It saved him putting it into words.

'It is.' There was a silence as they both dealt with their thoughts and then Jock spoke. 'Go on, say it.'

'There's no need.'

Jock picked up his glass paperweight and turned it in his palm, looking at the colours of the glass inside the heavy half-moon but not seeing them. 'There's every need. A fool and his money are easily parted, so the least you can do is say, "I told you so." Since you did, in no uncertain terms, as I recall.'

He heard Jules's sigh of exasperation but wasn't sure who it was aimed at. Probably both her brothers. There was no doubt in her eyes—and his, too—that older and younger were equally to blame.

'I told you Chris was a bad risk but I do understand, Jock. You've been taking care of both of us since we were little. A habit of a lifetime. And it's part of who you are. I, for one, wouldn't change a bit of you. Although…' her tone went dry '…I might say differently when we're both squished up together, sleeping on a park bench.'

Jock managed a laugh, but only just. 'I don't think it'll come to that. We won't be destitute but, bloody hell, it's going to be hard to let that place go.'

'I know. I just can't believe this is really happening—on top of everything else, too.'

He knew she was referring to the last six months, which had been anything but easy for her, forced to move in with him after a workplace injury had sentenced her to spending the next year or so doing rehabilitation. 'It's just one thing after another some-times, isn't it, when you're already fighting to get your unit opened and you've stuffed things up with Tilly.' True to form, she wasn't referring to her own experiences, she was thinking about him. He didn't deserve this sweet little sister and he hated laying this on her.

'There's more, Jules. It's already in the hands of an agent and they're coming over this afternoon so I need you to show them around.' He heard her intake of breath. 'Hell, I'm sorry, but they want to move fast. Reading between the lines, I think the bank or the agent, maybe both, already have a couple of buyers in mind.'

'It wouldn't be hard—it's an amazing property. Right on the most beautiful stretch of coast in all of Noosa.'

'Hold on,' Jock said, as a knock sounded on his office door and his secretary put her head around and motioned that Jock was needed. 'I'll have to go. Check in with me when the agents have gone and ring if you have any problems while they're there, although they sounded fine on the phone.'

She agreed and said goodbye. Just before she hung up, Jock muttered, 'I'm sorry, sweetheart,' but he couldn't be sure she'd heard.

The rest of the morning passed in the usual blur of work activity, with Jock heading for the phone every spare second he had to ring Chris again. By the end of the work day he'd still had no contact with his brother, which was lucky because the more time passed, the more livid he was becoming. If Chris walked through the doorway now, Jock thought as he shuffled papers around his desk in a vain attempt to get on top of his paperwork, he'd probably slug him.

Tilly said goodbye to her patient and took a moment to straighten some papers on her desk before calling the next patient in. She was still amazed at how quickly things between her and Jock had gone pear-shaped, how quickly the fires of passion had been doused by the blood ties of siblings. She didn't know if Jock had eventually looked for her last night and she'd called a taxi to take her to work, booking it for much earlier than Jock had arranged to collect her. She was doing a good job of avoiding the issue, too.

With everything they had going on in their separate lives, she wondered if they'd ever sort this difference out. Or if it even mattered.

If she wasn't planning on staying in Noosa then it probably made no difference, but if that was the case, why was she spending so much time dwelling on it? It was all because she wanted more of those kisses that had been about to lead her into trouble, making it hard for her to resume her old life when her time there was up. Well, she'd averted that problem now. She should be glad, but instead she felt like she was dragging a lead-filled body through the motions of her working day.

She picked up some casenotes, resolving not to think about Jock until the end of the day, and headed to the waiting room to call her next patient. 'Finn Patrick.' Tilly almost laughed when she saw a fair-headed toddler jump off his mother's lap and run across the waiting room, his full-leg cast barely inhibiting his pace. He'd altered his gait to accommodate the cast, swinging his right leg in an arc to clear the floor, and had obviously become used to the impediment.

Tilly squatted down to greet him, resolved to focus on her job for now. The mess she'd made of things would keep. 'Hello, Finn. I'm Dr Tilly.' She rose to speak to Finn's mum. 'The cast hasn't slowed him down, then?' she said with a smile.

'No, unfortunately. He was quiet for the first week but now I don't think he even notices it. He's been running everywhere and kicking a ball with his brothers, too.'

Tilly started walking, leading them to a consulting room. 'One assumes, then, that his fracture must be healing well.'

'I hope so.'

The clerk had left Finn's X-rays on the desk and Tilly removed them, selecting the most recent to put on the light box. A pale white line was visible across the top of the right tibia, just beneath the tibial condyles, indicating new bone growth across the fracture site.

'This all looks good.' She turned to Finn. 'Your leg's all better. Would you like me to take your cast off?'

He shook his head.

'Don't you want the doctor to take it off so you can go swimming again?'

His mother's question got a nod in response.

'Can you sit on the bed for me, Finn? Pop your legs up, too.' Tilly waited for his mother to lift him up and get him settled. 'OK, I'll get you to sit behind him for support. Finn, do your brothers like pizza?' He nodded again as Tilly picked up the electric saw, which looked like an oversized pizza cutter. 'Does Mum use one of these to cut the pizza? I'm going to take the front of your cast off with this, a bit like taking the lid off a box. I need you to sit as still as you can. This will be a bit noisy.'

Tilly switched the machine on, the noise loud enough to put an end to any conversation. In a few minutes she'd cut down both sides of the cast and was able to turn the implement off. Finn hadn't moved at all or made a sound, but when Tilly looked at him he had two big tears rolling down his cheeks. His mother wiped his tears as Tilly separated the two halves of the cast, removing it from his leg.

'What a brave boy! We're all finished. Can you bend your knee for me?' Tilly watched as Finn bent his knee without any sign of discomfort or restriction. 'Well done.' She inclined her head towards a glass lolly jar, silently getting permission from Finn's mum, who nodded her head. 'Would you like to come over here and choose a jelly snake?' The toddler climbed down from the table and crossed the room, showing no signs of favouring his right leg, just as she'd hoped. Tilly waited as he chose two snakes, one for each hand, and while he was engrossed with those she was able to talk to his mother.

'It's almost as if he's forgotten he was ever in a cast!' his mum exclaimed.

'Kids are very resilient.'

'They're amazing, aren't they? Do you have children?'

Tilly shook her head. She was used to this question. Most parents seemed to assume that a doctor working in paediatrics must be a parent. She knew sometimes the parents wanted to reassure themselves that Tilly understood what they were going through, and on occasion Tilly felt, despite all her years of training, no amount of theory could make up for the practical experience she was lacking.

But she'd spent her teenage and adult life being responsible, trying to prove to her grandparents she wasn't like her mother, that she was focused on serious goals, on a life filled with meaningful work. There was no way she was going to have children and sacrifice everything she'd built up. And beneath that she knew she'd never do it for another reason. What if she did and found out she was as incapable of raising a child as her mother had proved to be? There would be no going back then, and there would be no one to pick up the pieces if Tilly made the same colossal mistake as her mum had.

Finn's mother was still talking. 'Having kids is the best thing I've ever done. The hardest, too, but even on the really difficult days I wouldn't trade them for the world. The best advice I ever got was not to think about it because there's never a perfect time to have kids—just do it. And once you have them, you wonder what you were waiting for anyway. Nothing else will ever seem as important.' She stopped, pausing for breath. 'Sorry, I'm getting carried away. I don't want to make you run late. Do we need to do anything special now? Does he need physio or a follow-up appointment?'

'No. Generally at this age children will resume normal activity and that's enough exercise to ensure that they recover their muscle strength and range of movement. If he starts to favour that leg for more than twenty-four hours, you can bring him back in but looking at his movement already I doubt that will happen.

There's a small chance that his right leg may grow out at a slight angle—keep an eye on it compared to his left leg over the next twelve months—but it's not common.'

'What would we do then?'

'Take an X-ray to check the degree of difference and treatment would depend on the severity. Usually nothing is required and, as I said, it's very uncommon but you need to be aware of it.'

'Can he go back on the trampoline?'

Tilly had seen in the casenotes that Finn had fractured his leg while jumping on the trampoline. She hated to think of the number of children who presented in hospital every year with injuries sustained from trampolines, but she knew kids loved them. She'd loved them herself before she'd started studying medicine and seen the consequences.

'I'd wait another ten days to give his muscles time to build up and time for the bone to solidify, but after that I don't suppose you'll be able to keep him off if he's confident about jumping.'

'I was tempted to get rid of it after this accident but the boys use it almost continuously and it's a great way for them to use up some of their energy. I'll be enforcing our "one at a time" rule, though.'

'Probably wise. Trampoline injuries are the highest-ranking sporting injury in casualty departments for the under-eight age group. Children need to take care.' Tilly couldn't resist giving some warning as she saw them out, even though she could see the benefit of the trampoline to this family probably outweighed the risk.

As she walked them out to the reception area, she couldn't stop herself from glancing around for Jock. She grimaced. So much for not thinking about him until the end of the day. But their disagreement was weighing heavily on her mind, despite trying to tell herself it didn't matter, and she added this concern to her apprehension about her own health. Although her symptoms seemed to be lessening and her anxiety was easing, it wasn't completely gone. She was still waiting for a call from Dr Jones in Brisbane with her test results, and every time her phone rang she found herself snatching the handset from the cradle with lightning speed.

She had two more patients before lunch, both very straight-forward. First was a twelve-year-old girl for review of her asthma management plan and then a four-year-old girl with recurrent ear infections. Tilly organised a referral to the ENT specialist with a follow-up with her own GP in one week, but her thoughts kept drifting back to Finn.

Or, more precisely, to his mother's comments. She always shelved any thoughts of having her own children before they even took form. She knew it was for fear of failing to do it right, fear of repeating her mother's mistakes, but was she missing out on one of life's best experiences purely because of what might be rather than what would be?

The phone call from Andrea Jones finally came just before lunch, distracting her from further pointless self-examination. She'd made up her mind years back. Career, not children.

'I've got your test results back,' Andrea said.

'And?'

'Your blood test was relatively normal. Glucose and iron levels were within normal limits and no signs of viral infection.'

'What about the X-rays and urine test?'

'Protein was a bit elevated but nothing else. X-rays were clear.'

'So what's going on? Do you have any ideas?' Tilly held her breath.

'It might still be your neck, perhaps some residual ligament damage from the car accident. Can you organise some physio-therapy treatment to see if that helps?'

'What do I tell them?' She crossed her fingers, hoping that would be the easy solution.

'I'll send your X-rays up to you with a report, but your symptoms could stem from muscle spasm so I think it would be wise to have a physiotherapy examination. I'm also considering vertebro-basilar insufficiency, but I'll need to order another lot of X-rays with different views.'

Tilly pulled a face. 'I hope it's not VBI. '

'I agree. Make a physio appointment after the X-rays, send me the contact details and I'll fax my report and get the physio to ring me after your appointment. How have you been over the weekend?'

'Actually, I've been fine. I was hoping I'd turned the corner.'

'I'd be surprised, but stranger things have happened. I'll talk to you after the physio but ring me if you're worried about anything in the meantime.'

Did that include boyfriend problems? thought Tilly as Andrea hung up, leaving Tilly, phone beeping in hand, stunned as the thought caught her off guard. Since when had she thought of Jock as her boyfriend? He was just the man she'd been kissing, the man she'd managed to lose her head over for a few days, yes, but nothing more.

Whether there was a word to describe Jock—or whether there had been one before she'd offended him—was a dilemma she had to put to one side within an hour or so. By mid-afternoon the onset of another headache hit her hard. It was the worst one yet, and she knew her earlier optimism about her return to good health had been misplaced.

Swallowing an anti-inflammatory tablet, she tried to work out if there was a particular trigger. If it was caused by a virus she'd expect the headache to be present twenty-four hours a day, the same if it had a true inflammatory cause. Was it a mechanical problem, related to her posture or movements, causing muscle spasm? But her day-to-day activities hadn't changed significantly. Maybe the headache was present all the time as low-level pain and she only noticed it when it increased in severity? She went round and round in circles and got no further with her self-diagnosis. All she knew for sure was that these headaches were not normal and she'd taken to carrying pills around in her handbag, something she'd never had to do before.

And it was worse by the time she'd finished work. To add insult to injury, her self-imposed time limit for not thinking about Jock had ended, but she had no energy to turn her mind to that issue. She was about to call for a taxi when there was a knock on her door and Jock appeared. 'Have you got a minute?'

She nodded and put a hand to her temple to still the pain that shot through her head at the sudden movement. A wave of nausea surged up and she could scarcely muster hope or curiosity as to why Jock was there.

'I came to apologise for what happened yesterday. I know some of what you said was valid but Chris is my brother, my flesh and blood, and I won't ever turn my back on my siblings. That doesn't mean I agree with everything he does, but I don't ever want to let him down, not if I can possibly avoid it.'

'Jock, I appreciate your apology and I owe you one, too, but, to be honest, I'm having a hard time stringing two words together. Do you think we can take this up another time?'

Tilly couldn't believe she was asking that. All day, all she'd wanted had been a chance to clear the air but now she couldn't think straight. She just wanted to get home and lie down.

'What's the matter? Are you sick?'

She started to shake her head but stopped as another sharp pain pierced her skull. She covered her left eye with her hand, supporting her head. 'Just a ripper of a headache.'

'Any other symptoms—dizziness, nausea, shortness of breath?' Jock got straight to the point.

'No. I just need to go to bed. I'll be fine in the morning.'

'I'll drive you. Is Flo at home?'

'She's at the sewing circle. They've started making gifts for the hospital Christmas fair.' It was an effort to talk.

'Tell you what, I'll just swing past home and drop off some things Julianne's expecting, then I'll stay with you till Flo gets back.'

'That's not necessary.'

'No arguments. I want to do this, especially after yesterday. I wouldn't feel right leaving you alone. Besides, you need someone to tuck you into bed and bring you a hot-water bottle.'

That did sound good. 'OK, thank you.'

She let him gather her bag and take her by the arm to lead her to the car park. She closed her eyes the moment she'd done her seat belt up and concentrated on keeping her head as still as possible. Every slight bump in the road was hellish, though she could tell he was driving more slowly than usual.

Eventually, she felt them turn off the bitumen onto Jock's dirt driveway, and he slowed even more. She could tell he was trying to avoid as many bumps and potholes as he could, before finally coming to a halt.

'I'll only be a minute. Do you want to wait here?'

'Yes,' was all she could say.

She heard Jock get out of the car, felt the cool air flowing in as he'd left his door ajar, could hear the dogs coming straight over, panting as they stuck their great big heads into the car to see who else was there. She didn't want them there but couldn't summon the energy to tell them to get away. Even when they started their crazy barking, the noise slicing through her skull, she couldn't tell them to stop. She sat in the car in a daze. She could feel them still by the open door but the noise stopped.

She forced her head to turn to them and opened her eyes to see why they'd gone quiet, but they were still barking. They were behaving more wildly, jumping on each other, jostling as they watched her, but she felt as if she was watching a movie on mute. Batman had backed out of the car and was leaping up and down, all four paws clearing the ground, and Robin was turning in circles, his jaw moving as he barked soundlessly. Tilly finally opened her mouth to tell them to be quiet but nothing came out.

Her mouth formed the words, she could feel it working, but her intention and her ability were not connected.

She'd lost the power of speech.

She needed to find Jock, needed to get out of the car, but her limbs weren't obeying her brain either.

Why couldn't she move?

A stroke—that was the only answer that whizzed through her panicked mind. She'd had a stroke. And she was going to die.

CHAPTER NINE

'BATMAN! Robin! Cut it out.'

Jock could hear them carrying on from inside. The noise would be agony to someone with a headache, so why wasn't Tilly pulling them into line? He came out of the house, saw the dogs by the car and wondered again why Tilly was putting up with the noise. Then he saw the problem.

Tilly was in the car but her body was jerking, spasms ripping through her.

He ran, covering the distance in seconds. The dogs were quiet now that he'd come. They'd been sounding a warning. A warning he'd ignored.

He yelled for Jules.

No reply. He called again.

'Jules!'

'What?'

'Ambulance. Now. Tilly's having a seizure.'

He put his hands out onto the side of the car, narrowly stopping himself from slamming into it. He ripped Tilly's door open, reaching across her to undo her seat belt. Her head was thrashing around with each spasm and he had to keep his head back so they didn't collide. Her colour was OK, she was breathing. He suppressed his panic and waited until Tilly's muscles relaxed slightly between convulsions before he manoeuvred her out of the car and laid her on her side on the ground.

Her convulsions stopped thirty seconds later.

'Tilly? Can you hear me? Lie still. You've had a seizure. The ambulance is on its way.'

Tilly's eyes opened and found his.

'It's all right. I'm here.' His voice was soft as he tried to reassure her.

She closed her eyes again, her breathing slow and deep. She'd fallen asleep.

'The ambos are coming. What happened?' Jules was beside him.

'I'm not sure. She's had a seizure. It looked like a *grand mal*. Can you grab my medical bag from the boot? I need to check her vitals.'

Jock counted Tilly's respirations and her heart rate and then dug out his sphygmonamometer to check her blood pressure. Everything was within normal limits. If he hadn't seen her convulsing, he would have thought she'd just gone to sleep.

'I'll wait with her. Can you track down Flo? Tilly said something about a sewing circle.'

'That's at the Centenary Hall, I think. I'll find her. Shall I tell her to meet you at the hospital?'

He nodded. 'Tell her Tilly's OK. She'll be worried.'

Jock stayed by Tilly's side and kept up a monologue as he waited for the ambulance. He gave the paramedics the information he had, which was pretty sparse. Over the next hour he repeated it all again to the doctor on duty at the hospital and then to Flo. He declined to be the admitting doctor but found the subsequent waiting almost unbearable. Relinquishing control did not come easily. Waiting for answers was even harder.

A steady, rhythmic electronic beep penetrated Tilly's consciousness and she lay still, trying to place the sound. It wasn't her alarm clock but it was familiar. She opened her eyes. She was looking at a ceiling she didn't recognise, white, with tiny holes like a pegboard and fluorescent lighting. She turned her head towards the noise and finally figured it out. A heart-rate monitor. She moved her hand and felt the sensor attached to her index finger.

'Hello, sweetheart.'

The voice came from her right. 'Gran?' She instinctively turned her head towards Flo but stopped as she felt a sharp pain behind her left eye.

'I'm here, darling. How are you feeling?'

'I've been better. Where am I?'

'In hospital. You had a seizure.'

'What?'

'You were at my place, on your way home.' Tilly saw Jock then, leaning in the doorway as if he'd been there for a while. 'Batman and Robin were going crazy and I came back to the car and found you fitting.'

'I remember the dogs going a bit strange. That's it, though. What happened?'

'We're not sure exactly. It looked like a typical epileptic seizure. We did an EEG while you were sleeping and the background frequencies were normal.'

'How long have I been asleep?'

'A couple of hours. We're waiting for the radiographer on call to come back in to take a CT scan.'

'We?'

'You're under the care of Susan Milne. I thought it would be better if I wasn't your treating doctor.'

'I haven't met Susan before, have I?'

'No, but she'll be along in a minute.' Jock tailed off as a nurse appeared in the doorway.

'The radiographer's here. We can take Dr Watson down to X-Ray.'

A sheen of sweat was breaking out on her forehead and her hands were clammy. Nerves. This whole episode had taken her by surprise and she was being whisked off for tests for which she hadn't had time to prepare. She made a mental note to ensure her patients had sufficient time to digest information in the future. She turned to Flo. 'Will you wait for me?'

Flo rose from her chair, kissing Tilly's forehead. 'Of course. I'll be right here.'

Tilly couldn't remember the last time her grandmother had kissed her voluntarily. Something strange was happening but she had no time to ponder this before two nurses she didn't recognise bustled in, unlocking the brakes on her bed and disconnecting her from the monitors, before wheeling her from the room. She wanted to ask Jock to go with her but her mouth was dry and she couldn't form the words. She was out of her room now, heading feet first along the corridor.

She lay on her back, watching the ceiling, counting the fluorescent lights as they slid past, trying to keep her mind blank. She'd never been admitted to hospital before, had never been a patient, and she was finding it an unpleasant sensation. She swallowed nervously and then saw Jock, walking beside her, smiling down at her. She felt his hand cover hers, his fingers tucked under her palm as he squeezed it gently, reassuringly. She was able to breathe again then, comforted by his presence and grateful he'd known without words how much she needed his support.

As she saw the sign for the radiology department she heard an unfamiliar voice beside her. 'Hello, Tilly. I'm Susan Milne.'

Her doctor. This was real. Even Jock's touch wasn't enough to block out that thought. She was a patient and she was about to have a CT scan to investigate her unexplained seizures. Tilly closed her eyes. She wasn't ready for this. Not one bit.

She heard the automatic doors at the entrance to Radiology slide open. Felt Jock squeeze her hand again. She knew she had to open her eyes. Susan was waiting to speak to her, but it took a concerted effort to force her eyelids apart.

She looked properly at Susan this time. She was short, about a foot shorter than Jock, and her curly brown hair was short, too. Her eyes had a gentle expression and when she spoke her voice was quiet and confident. Tilly started to relax.

'Tilly, I don't know whether Jock's explained to you. I'm a private physician and until we get some answers about what's happening to you we thought it would be best if I co-ordinated your care. Is that OK with you?'

Tilly nodded.

'Your EEG was unremarkable so I've organised a CT scan. With no history of epilepsy, we need to find out what caused the seizures.'

Tilly found her voice. 'What do you think you'll find?' She couldn't bring herself to ask the question that had formed the moment Jock had told her what had happened.

'I'm not sure. It could be a small bleed, an infection of sorts.' Tilly saw Susan hesitate and knew what was coming. 'Or it could be a tumour. The sooner we get this scan taken, the sooner we'll have some answers.'

Tilly nodded. What other choice did she have?

Jock was still holding her hand and he bent his head to hers. 'I'll wait in the viewing room. You'll be fine.' He said the right words but Tilly could see he was worried—the little crease between his eyes gave him away. She reached up, touching his frown with her fingers, trying to smooth it away. She didn't want him to be worried about her—she couldn't bear to think he had reason to be worried. She wanted him to pick her up and carry her out of there, away from Radiology, away from the hospital, away from this nightmare.

He brushed a kiss across her lips. 'I'll see you in a minute.'

He certainly wasn't hiding his affection for her today. That bothered her, too. Did that mean he thought she was really in trouble?

Tilly lay still as the radiographer introduced herself and explained the procedure. Tilly had never had a CT scan and knew she should listen. Knowing the theory behind it was bound to be different to actually experiencing it. She feigned interest, hoping she at least looked as if she was paying attention, but all she could really concentrate on were the two words Susan had spoken. Epilepsy. Tumour. What a choice.

She was transferred onto the narrow bed. She was tall but she wasn't carrying any extra weight yet she still felt as if she was going to fall off the edge. She closed her eyes as she was strapped into position, resisting the urge to fight against the belts. The bed was pushed into the machine and she heard the whirr of the motor as the drum started to revolve around her. She kept her eyes tightly closed, not wanting to see the confined space she was in. She was cold and it was hard to make herself lie still. Only the thought that if she wriggled they'd have to start again kept her from fidgeting. The noise was less than she'd expected which was the only good thing she could say about the whole experience. Finally the machine stopped and she was pulled out and the straps undone. She sat up, bracing herself for whatever Susan might have to say.

She could see the radiologist in the viewing room but it was Susan and Jock who came out to speak to her. That was good. She wasn't in the mood to meet any more new people. Doctors particularly.

'The film still has to be processed so I can't show you anything yet, but there is a small opaque spot, about the size of my fingernail, just here.' Susan touched the left side of Tilly's head, just above and behind her ear.

Tilly felt sick. 'That's where my headaches originate.' She wrapped her arms around herself and shivered. She was still cold.

'I'm not sure exactly what the spot is. I want to get a neurologist I know in Brisbane, Paul Baxter, to have a look. Do you know him?'

Tilly shook her head. She didn't want to hear any more. She knew the spot could be caused by a number of things but she didn't want to hear about them, think about them or talk about them. She just wanted it all to go away.

'Don't worry, we'll get to the bottom of this.'

Don't worry! What a useless expression she now knew that to be, but she'd said it to patients herself a thousand times.

Jock sat beside her, wrapping his arm around her and pulling her close.

'I'm scared, Jock,' she whispered.

'I know.' His voice was just as quiet. 'Come on, I'll grab a wheelchair and take you back to your room.'

Jock helped her off the bed, settling her into the wheelchair. She waited until they were out of Radiology before asking, 'What do I tell Gran?'

'Tell her you're waiting to hear from the specialists in Brisbane. She'll be happy as long as she knows it's being investigated.'

'Do you think I'll have to stay in here overnight? I should have asked Susan if I could go home.'

'I think Susan would prefer you to stay. She's worried about Flo coping with you alone. Stay overnight, for Flo's sake, just until Susan's had a chance to get some other opinions.'

'I don't want to be by myself.'

'What if I organise an extra bed for Flo?'

Tilly couldn't imagine her grandmother agreeing to sleep overnight in the hospital, but she was too weary to say anything. All she could manage was, 'Thank you.'

Letting Jock take charge was comforting, especially when she didn't have the energy to take control. A thought flashed through her mind that they'd been arguing but she couldn't make the thought stay in her head for long enough to remember what they'd argued about. Maybe they had resolved their differences and she just didn't recall. Regardless, Jock seemed to genuinely want to help. Although, if she knew one thing about him by now, it was that he would always offer assistance.

Aided by sleeping tablets, Tilly nodded off before Jock had organised an extra bed for Flo. He was rearranging a couple of chairs and the table to fit the bed into the room when Flo interrupted.

'Can I ask you a question?' He nodded. 'What do you think the spot is on the CT scan?'

He put a chair down before answering. 'It's almost impossible to say at this stage. We really need to get some test results back. Then, by a process of elimination, we'll be able to come up with a cause.'

'Could it be a tumour?'

There was no point pretending otherwise. 'It could be, but it could also be unrelated to her symptoms. Susan will keep investigating until we get answers. I promise we'll find out what's going on.'

'She's all the family I have left.' In her typical manner Flo was being direct and understated, and Jock found that easier to deal with than the tears and hysteria relatives often displayed. 'Losing her is not an option.'

Jock took another look at the older lady. Was that a trace of a tremor he'd detected in her voice? But her gaze was steady, a challenge to him to ensure her granddaughter was fine.

'I'll do everything I can.'

'I know you will.'

Jock glanced at Flo, waiting to see if she had anything further to say, but she was looking at Tilly now, lost in her own thoughts. For the first time Jock could see the link between the two women. Tilly had Flo's height and stature, back ramrod straight, proud, and proud to stand alone. But it occurred to him that for all Tilly's arguments at lunch the previous day, it had been him who had got it right. When disaster struck, family stood by you. Would she really cling stubbornly to independence and refuse help from those around her?

Tilly struggled to open her eyes, although she knew by the light filtering through her eyelids that it was well and truly morning. She felt tired and groggy, which was unusual. She was normally a morning person. The unfamiliar surroundings brought it all back—she was still in hospital and it was the after-effects of the sleeping tablets she'd taken making her feel out of sorts.

'Good morning. How are you feeling?' Flo was sitting in the armchair, the bed she'd slept on beside Tilly already packed away. Tilly's first impression was that she'd never seen Flo looking rumpled before, even though the traces of a night on a folding bed were only slight, and she found it disconcerting.

'I'm not sure yet,' Tilly replied. Actually, she felt agitated. The medication had affected her dreams and she'd spent the night haunted by surreal visions, or so it felt. 'What time is it?'

'Just after seven-thirty.'

'Have you been here all night?'

Flo nodded. 'I couldn't go home, not without knowing what was happening to you.'

Tilly was amazed. That was far from the no-nonsense behaviour she'd learned to expect. 'Have Susan or Jock been in yet?'

'Jock's only just left to get ready for work—he was here most of the night. I haven't seen Dr Milne yet.'

Hearing that Jock had also stayed the night stunned Tilly but calmed her, too. Still, it wasn't enough to block out the remnants of her dreams. She'd finally remembered what they'd been arguing about before she'd gone to sleep last night and had spent the night with her dreams disturbed by continuing replays of the event in all its rich, embarrassing glory. She cringed now when she thought of how Jock had held her hand yesterday, despite the awful things she'd said.

'I assume there's no news, then.'

'So it would seem. I'll wait for Dr Milne with you. Good news or bad, you won't hear it alone.'

'I'm sorry about this, Gran. You must have had quite a shock to hear I was in hospital, especially so soon after Grandpa...' Tilly's voice trailed off.

Her grandmother patted her hand in a comforting gesture, something Tilly didn't think she'd ever done before, not even when she'd been little and had broken her foot when she'd jumped out of a tree. 'All that matters is getting you better. You are the only family I have left and I'm not about to lose you.'

'What if I'm not going to be all right?' But from the look on Flo's face, she wasn't going to let that happen.

'Tilly Watson, if there's one thing I know about you, it's that when the world collapses, you'll be the last one standing. You're tough. You're a Macdonald through and through,' she said, citing her own maiden name.

Her gran was comparing them? Favourably? 'You think I'm strong?'

'Naturally,' she said in her no-nonsense way. 'You're just like me.'

'I am? I always thought *you* thought I was just like my mum.'

'To look at, yes, but she was much more like your grandfather, although she was more easily led than him and looked a lot more to others to make her feel good about herself. Whereas we,' she said, gesturing to Tilly and herself, 'can find our own way in the world. We don't need other people's approval and acceptance.'

Tilly was quiet for a moment, taking that in. Her gran was right, in some ways she'd never thought about. 'Except for one thing, Gran.' She swallowed, steeling herself to go on with the unfamiliar emotional revelation. 'I've always needed your approval.'

'No, Tilly, you might have thought you did, but you've always taken your own counsel first.'

Had she? She was going to question her further but Flo went on, 'Besides, you've always had my approval. And my admiration.'

Tilly felt her jaw drop. 'But I always felt I had to prove to you I wasn't like my mum, that I was responsible, independent, *successful,*' she protested.

'I loved your mum very much but she never did anything in her adult life I could respect. Other than making the decision to keep you, of course. That took determination, but then she couldn't cope with the responsibility in the end.'

'You loved Mum?'

'Of course.' Flo was giving her a very puzzled look. 'Why ever would you think otherwise?'

'You never speak of her and you always pushed me to be independent, to be her opposite.'

'Is that any wonder? I made many mistakes with her and I wasn't going to make them again with you—let you get away with anything without lifting a finger. Your grandpa indulged her and I was too busy running the station to step in. It seemed easier, they were so happy together. But that didn't mean I didn't love her,' she said. Then she looked very closely at Tilly and added, 'Or you.' She paused. 'Is that what this is all about?'

'I'm not sure. This is all news to me.' Tilly was quiet for a moment, processing her thoughts. 'I think you're right. I'd have been the way I am anyway, driven, looking for ways to find meaning in my life, feeling restless if I'm not achieving something. But I've also been chasing your approval.' She held out a hand to her grandmother, smiling when Flo hesitated then took it. 'And to hear you say I've always had it means a lot.'

'There's something else, isn't there? You're scared about what they're going to find?'

Tilly hesitated and then nodded. 'That's partly it.'

Flo continued, 'I know I'm not the easiest person to talk to. Eunice has told me often enough over the years how hard I make it for people to get close,' she said as Tilly tried to take in this new, softer side of her grandmother. 'But you *can* talk to me.' She paused, looking a little uncertain. 'If you want.'

Tilly took a deep breath. Could she confide in Flo? She had to try, she needed to talk to someone and maybe Jock was right. Maybe family was the best she could do. 'What if I have cancer? What if I have cancer and I have to have chemotherapy and I can never have children?' Tilly stunned herself with her honesty.

'Children? You want children?' Flo was obviously as stunned as she was.

'I'm not sure. I might. They don't seem as terrifying any more.'

'Children as well as your career? Instead of it?'

'Yes. No.' Tilly clutched her head in her hands and pretended to scream. 'I don't know, Gran. I was always too scared to think about it. What if I was just like Mum and couldn't cope? So I chose work, partly to prove I wasn't like Mum, and now you tell me I never had to prove that and I don't know how I feel.' She met her grandmother's gaze and for the first time in her memory held it, and let her emotions speak with the look that passed between them, the concern and the love she saw in the older woman's eyes bringing a lump to her throat. She swallowed and went on, her voice cracking.

Flo reached out a tentative hand and touched Tilly on the forearm. 'I know it sounds trite, but everything will be OK. I've never met a stronger woman than you, Tilly.' She smiled and added, 'Although I'm a close second. So together we're invincible.'

Funny thing was, Tilly thought when Flo had gone home to shower, the moment her grandmother had said that, she'd believed her. It was continuing to believe it in her grand-mother's absence that was going to be the problem.

One magazine, much agony of self-reflection and two cups of tea later, Tilly had had enough of trying to stay positive and was starting to fidget, wondering when Dr Milne or Jock would make an appearance. At half past eight, but feeling more like it was midday, Susan arrived.

'Tilly, I've just finished a conference call with the neurologist and also Len Solerno. He's an oncologist.'

Tilly closed her eyes briefly and took a deep breath to try to slow her heart rate. An oncologist—that didn't sound like good news. She opened her eyes and forced herself to make eye contact with Susan. Forced herself to ask the question.

'What did they say?'

'Paul got Len involved because he suspected a tumour. Jock told me you've just had blood tests done as routine after your overseas posting. Len's looked at those and agreed that there doesn't seem to be anything sinister there. No indication of malignancy. But he hasn't ruled out a benign growth. He wants to organise some more tests.'

'What sort of tests?'

'More bloods, an MRI scan and possibly a biopsy.'

Tilly felt the blood drain from her face. Blood tests and a scan she could handle, but she didn't like the sound of a biopsy.

'When?'

'As soon as possible. Certainly the blood work and MRI could be done today.'

'But there could still be other causes. It's not limited to a tumour?'

'There could be lots of other causes, we just need to start eliminating them. I also want to run a few other tests following up on the seizure—liver and kidney functions mainly and CSF analysis. There are a few avenues to explore, which is a good thing, don't you think?'

Tilly didn't know what to think. Her brain didn't seem to be processing the information—it had frozen a few minutes earlier. Jock. She had to speak to Jock. He'd help her to make sense of this. But what exactly had Susan said? She had to make sure she was giving Jock the right information.

'What do you want to do first?'

'Take some more blood and then I'll organise the MRI to be done. I'd like to get a cerebrospinal fluid sample today, too.'

'Will you do a lumbar puncture?'

'Yes.'

Tilly cringed at the thought of a large needle being inserted into her spine but as much as she wanted to refuse the test she knew it was necessary.

'Would you like me to put you in touch with Len so you can speak to him?' Susan asked.

Tilly didn't want to talk to an oncologist, she didn't want to think about those consequences just yet. 'I'd rather wait until we've got some other results back. Is that reasonable?' And she wanted to talk to Jock first.

'Whatever you want in that regard is fine. Let me get a nurse to take the blood and I'll get the other tests under way.'

Tilly nodded. She'd get her blood taken and then find Jock. She really needed a sounding-board.

It was mid-morning before she had a chance to phone Jock but her call was diverted and no one was able to find him. She knew she couldn't expect him to spend every minute with her, he had plenty of people demanding his time, but she felt unaccountably lonely. She needed him. Someone had to help her make sense of everything.

CHAPTER TEN

HIS morning had been nothing short of appalling since he'd left Tilly's hospital room, Jock reflected as he put his head down and almost bolted for his office. He'd just finished his clinic, which had run an hour overtime and been wall-to-wall with uncooperative children and obstinate parents. Or had it been the other way around? If he could just get to his desk without being ambushed with something else to deal with, he might be able to turn his mind to all his other issues.

He managed to make it to his office, close the door and even sit down at his desk before his phone rang. Jules.

'The valuer from the bank has just arrived. It seems he was expecting you.'

'Damn, I'd forgotten all about him.' He'd made the appointment the previous day after the agent had viewed the property, but amidst everything going on with Tilly he had forgotten to note it down.

'Understandable. I thought you might have.'

'Tell him to start looking around and I'll be there as soon as I can.'

'I can handle it, Jock. I'm sure he doesn't really need either of us here.'

He paused. Jules was probably right but the property was his, he was Chris's guarantor and the property was the collateral. The bottom line was the responsibility was his, not Julianne's.

'I'm on my way.'

He put down the phone and swapped his pen for his car keys. As he locked his office door he heard his phone ringing again. He left it. The call would be diverted back to the switchboard. He'd get a message later.

Meanwhile, there went any chance of starting to organise the media to fight on his behalf for the final stage of the unit, not to mention his ever-present paperwork. And it would have to take priority over visiting Tilly, too. There was no way around it. Strange how things worked out. The only place he really wanted to be was with her—she needed him—and yet commitments and life got in the way. He'd be lucky to make it back there before that night, even though she was less than six hundred metres away from where he stood right now.

'What are you doing here? I said I'd manage.'

From the look on Jules's face, she thought he was mad to have come out. If she'd said as much, he'd probably even have agreed with her.

'I know you did, but this guy is expecting me. What's his name again?'

Jules pulled a business card out of her pocket and handed it over. Jock glanced at the name, refreshing his memory.

'Where is he?'

'He's gone over to the cottage.' She took him by the arm, halting him. 'Go back to work, or at least to see Tilly. I can take care of it.'

He shook his head. 'This is my mess, not yours. I don't expect you to deal with it.'

'But you expect to fix everyone else's messes.'

'I don't.'

'You do. You're in this situation because you can't refuse to help. Although by now you should have learnt that Chris in particular is never going to learn to fend for himself while he knows you're around to bail him out. And look at me. I'm living in a cottage you could be renting out, living free of charge on your property with no responsibilities while I focus on my rehab. I'm just as bad as Chris.'

'You and Chris are completely different. I'm just helping you get back on your feet. I haven't done much for you.' Unlike what he'd done for Chris. He knew he was too forgiving and didn't demand enough from his younger brother, but what else could he do? He was family.

'That's not true. You've been looking out for both of us for thirty years. Who's looking out for you?' Jules demanded.

'I don't need anyone.'

'Rubbish. Everybody needs someone. How's Tilly doing?'

He ran his fingers through his hair. 'I haven't had time to see her today and the way things are going, I won't be seeing her any time soon.'

'You're out here when you could have been spending some time with Tilly?' Jules raised her voice. 'Are you crazy? It's time you started thinking about yourself, doing something you want to do instead of what you think you should do or what others expect you to.'

He couldn't agree more. The last place he wanted to be was at home, a home that might not be his for much longer. He should never have offered to help Chris again, but he couldn't imagine ever denying assistance to his siblings. He really wanted to be with Tilly but she would have to understand.

If he didn't want to face up to his mistakes, how could he ask Jules to do it in his place? This was the only option—if his home was going to be sold from under him, he had to be there.

Jock could see the valuer returning from the cottage. 'Can we discuss this later?' He spoke through gritted teeth as he put his arm around his sister and started walking towards the other man, the man who would be selling his home.

* * *

Jock sighed as he sat back down at his desk two hours later, looking at the mountain of paperwork that seemed to have expanded while he'd been with the valuer, and wondered where to start. He rubbed his eyes. He had a stress headache. He wasn't used to feeling like he had too many things on the go. He thrived under pressure but today he was finding out how it felt to be overwhelmed. Tilly. Chris. The bank. Juggling patients and paperwork. The unit. He'd kept today free for paperwork but he was having difficulty making inroads. He'd had to see some of the patients who would have been on Tilly's list, and when he had finally been free, there had been too many thoughts racing through his head. *Too many responsibilities.*

He picked up his pen, preparing to sign yet another stack of letters that seemed to be appearing on his desk every time he so much as blinked. Maybe after he did this he could duck out to see Tilly. It was well after four now and he hadn't managed to see her since he'd left that morning while she'd still been sleeping. Half an hour and seven unwanted phone calls later, he was striding down the corridor, heading for Tilly's room. She was alone when he entered.

'Am I glad to see you.' She looked pale and drawn but she was smiling.

'I've been trying to get back here all day. It's been chaotic, to say the least.' He kissed her cheek, looking closely at her.

'Is everything OK?' She was studying him closely, too.

'Everything's fine.' Or it would be. 'Where's Flo?'

'I sent her off to have a coffee with Eunice. She needed a break from here, not that she'd admit it.'

'Eunice is here?'

Tilly's smile was wry. 'I think I scared everyone with the seizure.'

'Me included.' There, he'd admitted it now. Tilly's fit had frightened the life out of him. 'Has Susan been able to give you any answers?'

'Nothing I've wanted to hear. I've had an MRI, which was inconclusive, and kidney and liver function tests were normal.'

'So no definitive answers.'

Tilly shook her head. 'I'm about to go to Theatre for a spinal tap. They told me about two hours ago and I've been practically whimpering ever since.' She pulled a face. 'I've come to the realisation that I'm the opposite of brave. I'm a terrible patient.'

'They say doctors make the worst patients.'

'In my case, they're right. Not that you could call me patient. I'm dreadfully impatient for answers and then I don't want to hear what Susan has to tell me.'

'I haven't heard Susan complain about you yet.'

'She might by tonight. I've been a positive pain all day. I don't want to go for the spinal tap but I don't like the other options either. I thought Jules might hold my hand. She said she'll pop in later.'

'Jules?' He knew Jules had taken a liking to Tilly. It was clearly mutual and that was all well and good, but there was one thing he wanted to know. 'Why didn't you ask me?'

'I think you've done enough for me, especially considering my behaviour the other day.' Her expression was sheepish. 'It took me a while to remember the argument, but I owe you an apology. What happens between you and Chris is none of my business.'

He gave her a rueful smile. 'Our apologies were somewhat sidelined, weren't they?' She nodded. 'I'm sorry, too. It's a habit of a lifetime, protecting my siblings. A few of your comments were very accurate, truths I didn't want to acknowledge then, but I agree—I'm not helping Chris in the long run by constantly propping him up. If it makes you feel any better, Jules let me have it with both barrels after you left that day. She had a go at Chris, too, so he packed his bags and hot-footed it out of there to safety.' He smiled and crossed his fingers. 'So, the way I see it, we're square. And if I promise to reconsider my attitude towards Chris, may I come with you to hold your hand?'

She shook her head then winced. 'I keep forgetting I still have that headache. I can highly recommend intravenous pain relief but when I move my head too suddenly, it's a killer.' He reached over and took her hand as she squeezed her eyes shut as if to banish the headache, and she patted his hand with her own. 'Thanks for the offer, but you haven't got time to be holding my hand, literally or figuratively. Especially as you must be shouldering some of my caseload, too.' She looked at him for confirmation and he shrugged. 'I'll ask Jules.'

'No need. I'm coming.'

'But you could do something more constructive with your time.'

'Paperwork can wait.'

'But—'

'Another day is neither here nor there as far as paperwork goes.' He didn't need to spell out what was more important. He should have listened to Jules and been here hours ago. He wasn't going to let Tilly down again.

'I bet you wish they'd turn off my pain relief, then I wouldn't be half so argumentative.'

'It's crossed my mind.' He chuckled. Here she was, ill, sick with worry, and yet she'd managed to get the only smiles out of him he'd had so far that day.

Tilly was curled into the foetal position with her back to the door by the time Jock had gloved and gowned. Her back was turning orange as the anaethetist swabbed her skin with Betadine.

Jock walked around the bed, dragging a stool behind him. He put it near Tilly's head and sat down so he was at her eye level. She looked nervous. He held her hand, their fingers twined together. Over her shoulder he could see the doctor drawing up local anaesthetic.

'All right, Tilly, I'm just going to pop some local in now.'

Jock felt Tilly flinch as the needle stung her back. He gripped her hand more tightly and stroked her forehead, hoping to distract her. He knew once the anaesthetic had taken effect she wouldn't feel the rest of the procedure, but again he found it difficult to sit by and be so helpless. Offering comfort was as much as he could do and therefore he was determined to do that properly.

The large-bore needle was being inserted now into the space between the fourth and fifth lumbar vertebrae and the anaethetist continued to explain his movements.

'I'm just sliding the catheter in and then I'll collect the fluid. It'll take a few minutes so you'll need to keep as still as possible.'

They all waited silently as the fluid dripped out into the small vials, three in all.

'Well done, Tilly. I'll just remove the catheter and you're all set.' The doctor placed a small dressing over the wound, before asking Tilly to roll onto her back. 'I'm sure you know the most common complication following this procedure is a nasty headache so I want you to stay in a supine position to reduce this risk. Caffeine drinks also help.'

'That wasn't so bad, was it?' Jock said as the anaethetist disappeared to degown.

'I'll let you know when the local wears off.'

'Come on, let's get you back to your room and I'll get you a cola.' He walked beside her as the nurses wheeled her out of Theatre, tossing his gloves and gown into the bins on the way. 'Then I'd better get back to work. But I'll come past tonight. Will you be OK?'

'I'll be fine. Thanks, Jock.'

The night nurses were on duty when Jock returned. He poked his head around the door before entering Tilly's room. 'It's past visiting hours. Am I allowed in?'

'You're the golden boy. Who's going to tell you off?'

'You have a valid point there,' he said as he came further into the room.

'You're in a better mood.'

'I've just had the first bit of good news in a long time.'

He was smiling. Tilly's stomach turned somersaults. 'And?'

'I've got funding for the unit!'

'How did you manage that? What happened? You hadn't even started your campaign yet, had you?'

'I'd spoken once to the local newspaper, to their political journalist. She contacted the health minister for comment and he told her that Noosa General was getting the funding. She has it on record.'

'But how? Why?'

'Remember Alex Marshall? The boy who fell down the cliff?' Tilly nodded. 'Apparently, Minister Laurie is his uncle. Alex's mum is his sister. If we have the unit up and running when Alex is discharged from Brisbane it will mean that Ros can room in with him. Suddenly the minister is all in favour of the unit being completed.'

'Unbelievable. Does the man have no shame?'

'Right now I don't care why it's happened, I'm just glad to have the unit back on track. Seems like the old adage is true— it's not what you know, it's who you know.'

'Congratulations!' Jock was right, it was good news and she was happy for him. 'I agree, it's great to have something go your way. How long before you can start the final stage?'

'I'm going to get the ball rolling tomorrow. Hopefully it'll be completed in a couple of weeks. I'd really like to be able to bring Daisy and baby Jon back to the unit.'

'How are they doing? Any news about them?' Tilly felt a lump in her throat and swallowed, trying to get a handle on her emotions. Every time she heard babies mentioned now she got teary, much as she was trying to block those thoughts from her mind.

'Jon is doing really well. He's still in High Dependency but the doctors are expecting to transfer him soon. The risk of infection is their main concern now.'

Tilly's eyes were misty and she sniffed as her nose started to run.

'What's the matter? Is your head hurting?' Jock was beside her, concern etched in his features, his brow creased.

'No. I'm just a bit emotional, thinking about some of the mums and children I've come across lately, like Adam Davey and even Alex and his mum in the national park. When you mentioned Daisy Williams, it started me off again. And I've been talking to Gran about my mum. And about me.'

'And you're feeling sad? Worried?'

'It's all making me think about my mum, among other things.' She wasn't going to tell him about her fears concerning cancer, chemotherapy and the effect it might have on her child-bearing prospects, not when she'd been so adamant with him about not wanting children. It had been such a rapid change of heart that *she* hadn't even adjusted to the idea yet. 'I wish I'd had a chance to get to know her.'

'I didn't think you missed her,' he said, taking her hands between his and massaging them. His touch was soothing, encouraging her to confide in him.

'I miss the idea of her, I guess.' She rewarded his caresses with a watery smile. 'I'm blaming all the medication I'm on for being over-emotional. Those mums I mentioned, they'd do anything to protect their children and I wonder what that's like, to have that. And I realise now I'd have liked to know what she was like. All I know is what I've been told.'

'And what is that?'

'That I'm not like her after all, except in looks. I've spent my whole life trying to prove I wasn't irresponsible and immature like her, proving I could do more and do it better than anyone else. Now I find out not only did my grandmother never think I was like her, she loved my mum anyway, although she was disappointed in her and in herself for not raising her to be a stronger person. I've spent my whole life trying to ensure they had no reason to be disappointed in me, like they were with her.'

'You wouldn't have taken the path you have if you hadn't been trying to prove something to them?'

She mulled this over. 'N-o-o,' she said, drawing out the syllable while she thought. 'I still think I would have done that. I've loved my aid work. I'm not sure what it means exactly. But I think I would've felt less…alone…maybe just satisfied, if I'd known sooner they respected what I was doing, that I didn't have to prove anything to them.' She shook her head. 'Like I said, I'm really not sure yet what my chat with Gran has changed.'

'You've got a lot on your mind right now. What are you thinking about your mum now?'

'Maudlin, silly things.' She laughed, the sound jaded even to her own ears. 'Other than our looks, it turns out the only thing we might have in common could be dying young.'

'Look at me.' Jock was sitting on her bed in a second, letting go of her palms and clasping her face between his hands instead, making her look at him. 'You are not going to die.'

'Everyone dies eventually.'

'Eventually, but not yet. Not you. We'll get to the bottom of this.' He dropped a kiss on her forehead, then traced a finger over the skin. 'It's late and you're tired. You need to sleep. It will seem clearer in the morning.'

'That's such an odd saying.'

'Odd but true.'

He was right. She was exhausted. She didn't want to talk any more, didn't even want to think if she could help it.

'Do you want me to get the nurse to bring you a sedative?'

'No, but thanks.' She didn't want an artificial sleep. She closed her eyes as Jock kissed her goodnight, the touch brief but sweet on her lips, and as he left the room she tried to capture the feeling of his kiss, to lose herself in his kiss. Tried to believe he had the ability to chase all her fears away, to kiss her better. It almost worked.

* * *

Jock was right. With the dawn of a new day the fears that had been plaguing Tilly the previous day ebbed away and her normal optimism returned. Of course she'd be OK. And she'd prove it by getting out of there that day. Being a patient had already worn thin and when she heard Susan on the ward bright and early, she called out to her.

'Good morning,' said Susan. 'I was just coming in to see you. How did you sleep?'

'Like a log.'

'Have you had any reaction to the spinal tap? Any post-procedural headache?'

'No. I've had a few cans of cola and cups of tea and they seem to have done the trick. There's no trace of a headache and no other symptoms of any description either. I feel like a complete fraud.'

'Well, I can tell you you're not. I have your CSF analysis.'

Tilly's eyes were drawn to the papers clutched in Susan's hand and she felt as though a thousand butterflies had come to live in her stomach. 'And?'

'I have a diagnosis for you.'

CHAPTER ELEVEN

TILLY eyed the papers with suspicion. 'And what is it? What's wrong with me?'

'You have a neurocysticercosis.'

Tilly assumed she should know what that term meant but she was drawing a blank. 'A what?'

'A tapeworm.'

Should she feel disgusted or fortunate? She went with disbelief instead. 'I don't have a tumour? A brain tumour?'

'You don't.'

'You're definite?'

'Yes. It's not a diagnosis you'd choose to have, but perhaps it's better than the other options.'

Tilly nodded. That much she'd already concluded.

'How did you come up with the answer?'

'The CSF analysis indicated it, everything fits and everyone agrees. The white spot on your CT scan is a parasite with a surrounding inflammatory reaction.'

Feeling disgusted was already vying heavily with feeling fortunate. She'd have to switch into doctor mode so she could deal with this news. 'The inflammation is my immune system's reaction to the presence of a foreign body.'

Susan nodded. 'Yes, the body must be starting to deteriorate.

Your immune system has recognised it as foreign and so your body has started attacking it now.'

'And that caused the swelling, which led to the seizure?'

Susan nodded and Tilly ran her fingers over the area of her skull where the problem lay. Talk about it like it was happening to someone else, that was the way. 'What happens now?'

'Treatment is relatively straightforward. I've run through our approach with Andrea Jones in Brisbane. She seems to know the most about this sort of thing and is disappointed she didn't think of it earlier. She suggested we start you on an anticysticercal medication, albendazole, to kill any parasites.' She checked her notes. 'One 400 milligram tablet, twice daily for eight days. You'll also need high-dose glucocorticoids, probably Decadron, to manage complications for six days and anticonvulsant meds. We'll commence with Tegretol and see how you go.'

'That's it? Eight days of meds and I'm fine?'

Susan shook her head. 'Not quite so simple. The Tegretol needs to be continued for two to three months until we do a follow-up CT scan. If that looks clear, you'll come off all medication. It's a good prognosis.'

'What about side-effects?'

'You might experience some from the albendazole. There's quite a list.' Susan pulled a folded drug sheet from her coat pocket and started reading. 'Abdominal pain, nausea, vomiting, diarrhoea, dizziness, high temps, hair loss and increased intracranial pressure. You shouldn't experience all of those but you'll know you're on it.'

'It's still a lot more appealing than chemo.' Her optimism hadn't been misplaced. She'd be fine. If she hadn't been attached to her drip, she'd have danced a jig right this minute.

'No comparison. You may not have any side-effects at all but you should expect to experience a few to some degree.'

'I'll happily even take the worst ones. I'm just so glad it's not a tumour.'

The door opened and Tilly turned her head in that direction, wincing as the movement sent sharp pains through her skull again.

'Gran!'

Flo walked into the room, elegant as always even with the lack of sleep Tilly knew she'd been having. 'I hope I'm not interrupting, Dr Milne. One of the nurses said to come in.'

'Not at all. Tilly and I were discussing her diagnosis.'

Flo paled.

'It's good news, Gran, don't stress.'

Tilly filled her gran in on the diagnosis and her treatment plan, Flo looking just as worried as when she'd entered the room.

'Are you sure it's good news, Dr Milne?' she asked, her voice filled with doubt. 'It sounds a very nasty thing to me.'

Susan laughed. 'It does, and Tilly will be quite the curiosity on the ward until she goes home. But it's treatable and Tilly should be fine. In remote locations overseas it's not at all unusual, but it's rarely seen here so it's not an easy diagnosis to make.'

Her gran was still looking anxious. Tilly didn't blame her—it wouldn't sound great to someone who had no experience of parasites. It didn't sound all that wonderful to her. Like Andrea, she wondered how she could have failed to think of this herself, given all her years in the field.

'Will the fits stop?' Flo was looking from Susan to Tilly and back again, as if worried that something else would happen to Tilly right now if she took her eyes off her for more than a moment.

'Yes.' Susan addressed herself to Tilly. 'We'll start you on your medications now and your response should be almost immediate in terms of preventing further seizures.'

'How did she get it? Was she bitten by something?'

'Nothing as dramatic as that.' Susan hesitated and Tilly guessed she was debating whether it was wise to enter into a detailed description to Flo.

'I think Dr Milne is wondering whether you're up to hearing e gory details,' said Tilly.

Flo pulled herself up straighter. 'If it affects you, I want to know.'

'It's simple, like the acquisition of most parasites. Pigs harbour the tapeworm larvae. At some point Tilly has eaten poorly cooked, infected pork and consumed the larvae as well.'

'Yes, I get the picture,' said Flo, and Tilly suppressed a smile. She'd never seen her gran daunted by anything before. 'But how did one of the things end up there?' She pointed in the general direction of Tilly's head.

'The larvae end up in the intestinal tract and lay eggs. The eggs are able to pass through the gut wall into the bloodstream. One travelled…' She must have seen the greenish look coming over Flo's face, because she seemed to amend what she was going to say next, and instead waved a hand in the direction of Tilly's head, just as Flo has done a moment before. 'And became lodged in her brain. At some time it hatched and there it lived quite happily.'

'Why the brain?' Flo asked.

'They seem to have a preference for brain tissue but also eye, muscle and subcutaneous tissue. I doubt very much that this will be the only worm or larvae in Tilly's body.'

Tilly pulled a face. She agreed with her gran. It was all rather disgusting but part of her was intrigued and her need to know on a medical level was overriding the sense that it was her they were talking about. 'How long has it been there?'

Susan spread her hands. 'In larvae form it could have been there for months. Years, even.'

'No one eats pork in the province where I've spent most of the last two years.'

'Then it's entirely possible that it was there before that. You were in the Indian subcontinent for quite some time before Indonesia?'

Tilly nodded and Susan continued. 'From what Andrea tells me, it's prevalent in a large number of areas within that region. This parasite is dying now, which is what's triggered your body's immune system, but as I said, you probably have others, so you need to start the medication to kill them all.' Susan stepped away from Tilly's bed. 'I'll see you again in the next half-hour on rounds but I wanted to tell you before we had an audience. I'll have a larger entourage than usual, I warn you. Everyone will want to hear about you. We don't usually come across such an exotic case.'

'Hopefully the novelty value will wear off and you'll let me out of here.'

'Now that we know what we're dealing with, I'm happy for you to go home later today.'

Susan left the room and Tilly settled back against her pillows, shifting her drip line out the way and scratching her hand near where the Gelco was taped to her skin. 'These things are itchy,' she complained. 'At least now it can come out and I'll just have to swallow tablets instead.'

Flo leant across and kissed her cheek. 'Darling, you have no idea how glad I am you're going to be fine.'

'I have some idea, Gran. Believe me, I'm pretty relieved, too.'

'So no chemotherapy, I understood that right?'

'No chemotherapy.'

'So you can have my great-grandchildren.'

'Yes, Gran, when I work out if that is actually what I want and when I find someone who is interested in sharing that task with me, I'll let you know.'

'I'm not getting any younger and you've taken at least five years off my life in the last few days so, please, do hop to it, Tilly.'

'Are you telling me to skip marriage?'

'Tilly, I'm just so happy you're going to be fine that you could tell me you have five illegitimate children hidden some-where and I'd cry for joy.'

'OK,' said Tilly slowly. 'Are you *sure* you're all right?'

'Yes.' She picked up the phone and handed it to Tilly. 'So, enough with the pretence. Ring Jock and tell him you're going be fine.'

'Gran, he's frantic with work and…' she paused, not knowing how much her Gran knew of Jock's other crisis at present '…other things right now.'

'He'll be a lot less frantic when he knows you're going to be fine.'

So she dialled. 'He's not answering.'

Her door opened and medics swept into the room—twice as many as the preceding day.

Gran patted Tilly's hand. 'I'll come back after a coffee. Keep trying Jock.'

'I will.' Flo left the room before it was invaded by medical personnel all eager to have their professional curiosity sated.

Jock checked his watch before stepping through the automatic doors of the Suncoast Bank branch. 9.29 a.m. He had one minute to spare.

'You look terrible.'

'Jules.' His sister was there, and a welcome sight she was, too. 'You didn't need to come.'

She reached up to kiss him on the cheek and slipped something into his hand.

'I don't even need to look. Iced coffee. You…' he put an arm about her '…are a champion.'

'Thought you'd need it since you raced back to the hospital at first light.'

'You're right.'

'How is Tilly?' Jules asked.

'I didn't get time to see her. I was trying to catch up on some admin stuff.' He held up a hand to ward off the criticism he knew he was about to receive. 'But she is my top priority and I will be back by her side as soon as this is over.'

'I'm intending to go in myself later today, so I'll be checking up on you.' She wagged a finger at him. 'But for now, drink up—you need the caffeine hit.'

'Thanks. I don't think we'll be served coffee and biscuits

here, now that I've slipped from important investor status to pauper.'

'I thought you knew this Roan whoever-it-is we're meeting.'

He opened the carton and downed it in one long drink, just as a door opened and the business loans manager entered the foyer.

'I do. I'm joking about not being offered coffee but, believe me, you wouldn't want it. Foul stuff.' He tossed the empty container into a nearby bin before walking to meet the man coming towards them. 'He's here,' he told Jules.

'Roan,' he said as they shook hands, 'this is my sister, Julianne. Julianne, this is Roan Macquarie, the evil bank manager.'

Roan laughed. 'Pleased to meet you, Julianne,' he said as he shook her hand, too. She fell into step with Jock as Roan motioned them through to his office. He waited until they were seated opposite him at his desk before speaking again. 'Can I offer you a coffee?'

'Hell, no,' replied Jock.

Roan laughed. 'You're right. My caffeine intake has dropped right off since I came here. All right, then, we'll get started. I think I might have better news than you're expecting.'

'Good news would be very welcome today,' Jock replied although he held little to no hope of news good enough to brighten his day.

'I won't keep you in suspense. Land values around here have done well in the past two years. Skyrocketed might be a better term, particularly for land with water views or, better still, water access, which yours has.'

'Skyrocketed? What sort of figures are we talking about?'

'In some parts of Noosa a quarter-acre block of land is fetching well over six hundred thousand dollars.'

'For a vacant block!' Jock was stunned.

'There have been significant sales in the last eighteen months, more than enough for us to be confident of this assessment. The implications for you are that unless you want to capitalise on the market and sell your entire property, there's no need. It will be ample to subdivide a parcel for sale.'

'What size block are you talking about?' Jules asked, cutting straight to the chase.

'A quarter-acre allotment with beachfront access would be a very attractive proposition. You should get six, seven hundred thousand for that, which would more than cover what you owe.'

'And you think it's possible to get council approval for such a subdivision?' He wasn't willing to take a gamble on bureaucratic efficiency.

'There should be no problem with that,' Roan replied. 'It would be an even more attractive proposition if the land already had utilities connected. You'd get another hundred thousand or so if the allotment contained the cottage as well.'

'Who in their right mind would pay that amount?'

Jules kicked Jock under the table and widened her eyes at him when he sent her a look. Clearly, she wasn't impressed with his business strategy so far. Like he had one. That was why he was in this mess.

'Plenty of people.' Roan was nodding to underline his point. 'The bank would have several interested parties without even advertising. This sort of offering is very rare.'

'I'm not interested in including the cottage.'

'Can you excuse us for a moment?' Jules grabbed Jock's arm and dragged him out of the room, scarcely closing the door behind them before snarling at him, 'Have you gone completely mad? Ten minutes ago you thought you'd have to sell everything. Now he's telling you that you can keep most of it, including your own house, and you're refusing to sell the cottage!'

'The cottage is your home.'

'I don't care about the cottage. I'll find somewhere else to live and it's time I did. Did you actually hear what he was telling you? It's perfect.' Her grip on his arm was vice-like.

'I'm not kicking you out.' He was adamant about that.

'If you don't sell the cottage, I'll leave anyway. I've been trying to tell you I'm intent on turning things around for myself. The least you can do is let me.'

'What do you mean, you're turning things around for yourself?'

'Just that. We don't need to go into it now—just get back in there and tell him you'll go with the subdivision.'

Jock stood still, watching his sister's animated face as she tried to convince him she wanted to stand on her own two feet. She wasn't faking it. Something had changed and she was letting him know it was time to let go.

'Jock Kelly, you're the most stubborn...' She dropped her hand from his arm and gripped her hands into fists.

He watched as she searched for the right word to describe him. 'Ass?' he suggested.

'Whatever, you're the most stubborn one ever. You get back in there now and do as I say or I'll...I'll...'

The sight of his little sister trying so ineffectually to threaten him was the final straw. He couldn't help it. He folded up and laughed. 'You'll what, Jules? Haul me back in there all by yourself?'

She was glaring at him but he could tell she was about to laugh, too. They'd never been able to stay cross at each other for long. Not when for so many years it had been just the two of them, Jock and Jules against the world.

'If I have to,' she managed to get out before she also started laughing. 'OK, so you'd win but you still have to listen to me. You go back in there, sort it out then get back in your car and go and see Tilly.'

'You know, Jules, I can see now I should've started listening to you a long time ago when you first warned me about bailing Chris out. I wouldn't have got us into this mess if I had.'

'You'll do it?'

'On one condition.'

'What?'

'You agree you always have a home with me.'

'You just love me for my cooking.'

'There is that.'

She swatted him on the arm and gave him a shove in the back in the direction of the door. 'Go.'

'Are you coming?'

'And watch you sell my home from under me? Are you kidding?' At the look on his face Jules held her hands up. 'Really. I was kidding.'

'Come.' He grabbed her by the hand. 'Now all we need is good news about Tilly and everything will be right with the world.'

It took more than an hour before he'd signed all the appropriate documents authorising the bank to start proceedings. More than an hour before he could head back to the hospital. He'd thought he'd feel relieved once the mess with Chris was resolved, but the weight on his chest was still there.

He'd convinced himself that the major cause of his sleeplessness and constant worry lines was because of Chris—a result of his feelings of responsibility mixed with the emotions about losing his property—but, in the end, agreeing to the sale hadn't been difficult. Not that he'd really had a choice, but there had been no sharp pull when he'd given his verbal agreement to the sale. No despair as he'd signed instructions.

Somewhere over the course of the last few days, his feelings about Chris had shifted. Maybe it had been Jules's influence, maybe Tilly's, maybe just common sense catching up with him—finally—but he didn't think he even felt partially responsible for Chris any more. He searched his conscience while he drove and couldn't find guilt or anger at his brother anywhere in his heart. Sadness, yes; regret for not having helped him face up to himself earlier, yes. But not the overwhelming feeling of being responsible for his younger brother he'd carried around for close to thirty years.

But for all that, the heaviness in his chest was still there and as he turned into the hospital car park, the feeling worsened and then he knew.

The heaviness wasn't anxiety over his property.

It wasn't sadness or guilt or anger because of Chris.

There was no denying it. The leaden blocks still resting across his heart were there because of Tilly; the fear was there because of Tilly. Fool that he was, he'd refused to believe there was anything seriously wrong with her. He'd been in denial about her health.

And about what she'd come to mean to him. For the first time he wasn't at all sure blood was thicker than water.

He swung his car into his parking space and jerked on the handbrake. Within seconds he'd slammed the door and was striding, head down, towards Tilly's room.

She was going to get well.

That was all there was to it. He wouldn't accept anything less than that, he thought as he clenched his hands at his sides and stormed through the entrance as though the hospital itself had contrived to make Tilly sick.

Tilly was going to get well and he was going to tell her how he felt. He'd walk straight up to her, take her in his arms and tell her. Tell her he'd been worried sick about her but he'd not realised until now what she'd come to mean to him even in the short time they'd known each other. And now he knew, he wanted to be with her every moment he could and see what paths they might be able to travel together.

It was all going to be fine. No, not just fine.

Perfect.

But 'perfect' didn't allow for Tilly's room to be crammed with hospital staff when he entered.

And a chorus of 'Hi, Jock' wasn't the soundtrack he'd have chosen either.

But then there was Tilly. And *she* was perfect. He could just get a glimpse of her over the shoulders and between the heads of everyone else. She looked like she was craning to see him, which was close to perfect, too.

It didn't take long for the room to clear.

'The hospital grapevine is good for something,' he whispered to Tilly as the last nurse left the room and they were alone.

'Pardon?' She was smiling and looked as if she had a new lease of life.

'I wanted to see you. Alone. The gossip mill cleared the room for me.'

She didn't answer, just smiled and patted the bed. He sat at the edge, facing her, before he realised one concrete thing that was different.

'You've had your drip out.' And then it clicked and he shoved his half-prepared speech to the back of his mind. 'And your room was full of staff. Happy staff.' He glanced around like the answer might be in the room somewhere. 'What's happened?'

Then he looked back at her. She was still pale but she was smiling with pure relief and she looked beautiful, and he knew. 'You have a diagnosis.'

She nodded, beaming now.

'Want to share?'

'My diagnosis? Yes. What's actually wrong with me? No, you wouldn't want a share of that.'

'But it's good news.'

'It is. I have a neurocysticercosis.'

He knew what that was but he didn't know if he believed it. To say he was stunned was putting it mildly. He didn't know much about it, but he knew enough to know this was a far better outcome than the ones he'd been trying to ignore. In time, Tilly would be fine.

'That's it?'

'Well, I probably have more than one. Not nice but treatable.'

'What is the treatment?'

Tilly gave him as much information as she could recall.

'That diagnosis never even occurred to me,' he said.

'Nor me, although I feel now it should've.'

'If it didn't occur to the specialist in tropical diseases, I think we can let you off the hook.'

She shuddered. 'Don't talk about hooks, it reminds me of worms.'

He laughed. 'Don't tell me you scare so easily, Jungle Tilly.'

'I'm not scared of a parasite, I just don't care for them very much. Not when it's using me anyway. But if it means I can be discharged, I'm happy. I'd like to get back into the real world and be a doctor again, not a patient. What's been happening beyond these walls anyway? Anything I should know about?'

Now.

Now was the time to tell her how he felt. Tell her how worried he'd been.

He must have taken too long to answer because she jumped into the silence.

'What is it? Something's happened. Is it Chris?'

'No.' He rubbed at his eyes with a hand and felt weariness descend just thinking about what had been going on. Bone-tired was the expression that came to mind. 'There's a lot I need to fill you in on with that, but it can wait until you're a little stronger.'

'I'm fine. Really,' she added when he sent her a quizzical look. 'Have you sorted things out with Chris?' She was asking the obvious questions, assuming the cause of his trouble was the other problem, the brother factor. 'Is it going to be OK?'

He forced his mind to stay on topic. 'Yes, it is. I've just come from the bank and the upshot is that I've signed off a block of land, with the cottage, to be sold. It'll clear my debts.'

'But that's great news.' She was watching him closely. 'Isn't it?'

'Jules thinks so. And, yes, I'm actually fine with it, too.'

'Then what? You look like you've just lost your best friend.'

'I haven't lost anything that matters to me.' He steadied his nerves and picked up one of her hands between his. 'But I'm hoping I might have found something that matters a great deal.'

'Yes?' There was a look of expectation on her face and it gave him courage to speak. Courage to say what he'd never imagined saying.

'I realised today after I signed off on the land that it's been you causing me sleepless nights.'

'Me?' The certainty on her face was wavering.

'You.' He turned her hand over and traced a finger along the faint lines in her skin—the lifeline? The heart line? He didn't know the first thing about palmistry but it seemed absolutely right that his future could somehow be mapped out in the patterns on her soft skin. There was symmetry in that thought that, however crazy, made sense.

'We've only known each other a short time.' She was nodding—agreeing. Was it too short a time to be having these thoughts? He pressed on. 'I've never said this before, Tilly, never even felt it, but there's something there between us. If you hadn't become ill, it probably would've taken me a lot longer to recognise what's been staring me in the face since the moment I met you.

'I've been under a lot of pressure with the unit, Chris and the bank, but that's all resolved now and I expected the pressure to lift, but it hasn't. The pressure, the rotten feeling of being on a sinking ship and not being able to fight my way off was all to do with you. I hadn't let myself think that you were really ill. I convinced myself it would pass, that it was a minor blip. And then I realised it might be something more serious, something I was powerless to fix.'

'I didn't know you were so worried about me.'

'I didn't either.'

'So you haven't suffered for me at all?' Her grin was pure impishness and it was doing strange things to his heart.

'I did. I just didn't realise it was for you.'

'That's not quite as romantic as telling me you've been in the pits of agony, torturing yourself with thoughts that I might die.'

'You can't imagine how pleased I am to know you'll be fine. To think we're going to have time together.'

'I can imagine,' she said. He was still holding her hand and now she squeezed his fingers gently, reassuringly. 'I'm still on a high about the diagnosis, too. I've been convinced that I was going to...' Her eyes widened a little and she seemed hesitant to voice the word. 'To not be here for much longer, like I think I mentioned to you in one of my less upbeat moments. It's spun everything around. First I was thinking about all the things I want to do that I wasn't going to get a chance to, and now, in between endless streams of visitors, since I'm the new spectacle here, all I can think of is that I *am* going to get a chance. So one of the first things I'm going to do—'

She was interrupted when the door opened and a nurse entered the room.

'Excuse me, Dr Kelly, I thought Tilly was alone. I just need to do her discharge obs.'

Jock stood up as he said, 'Go ahead. I know Tilly doesn't want to be here a moment longer than she has to.'

The nurse pulled the chart from a rack at the end of the bed and Tilly dropped her voice to say, 'Can you stay? There are things I need to tell you.'

Jock checked his watch. 'I have clinic starting in five minutes and we're over-full as it is. I can't start late.' He stood up and dropped a kiss on her cheek. What he wanted to do was hold her, tell her what she meant to him and then kiss her thoroughly, but there was an impatient nurse waiting a metre away.

'I'll come to see you tonight if you're not too tired. I'll call first.'

'Don't call, just come.' There was an urgency about the look in her eyes, like she needed to know he'd be there, like she had something to tell him, too, that she couldn't wait any longer than necessary to say. He left her room with a spring in his step, a lightness that had been missing for a while. Everything *was* going to be perfect.

The high lasted exactly forty-five minutes: it ended between patients three and four when the ward clerk entered his room with a pile of mail.

'These are all for Dr Watson. I was going to send them down to her but she's been discharged. They said to give them to you.'

Jock wondered who 'they' were. Clearly, the hospital grapevine had once again left nothing unreported, but there seemed to be no fall-out from the news. His staff and colleagues seemed genuinely happy that something—whatever they thought that 'something' was—was happening between Tilly and himself.

'I'll get them to her.' He held out his hand, taking the stack to pack into his briefcase, and as the clerk closed the door behind him, he glanced at the pile. And then he saw it.

On top of the pile was a fax.

It was the letterhead that caught his eye. He'd seen it among Tilly's papers when she'd applied for her current position. It was from the aid organisation Tilly had worked for.

He read the sender's address details before he'd even registered he was prying. And once he had, he couldn't stop himself. His eyes skimmed the paragraphs below it and the words flashed up at him. 'Have received your message. Confirm twelve-month placement beginning May.' And it named a country in North Africa.

Tilly wasn't staying.

She was going back.

Not just going back. She'd signed on for a whole new chapter in her life.

How had he forgotten that her position here was temporary?

What had she said? 'I was thinking about all the things I want to do that I wasn't going to get a chance to…now…all I can think of is that I *am* going to get a chance.' And she'd emphasised it less than an hour before: she couldn't wait to get back to her work as a doctor.

The plans she had for her future didn't include him past the next couple of months. She was clearly responsive to him, but it was a short-term thing, like everything had been in her life—her parents, her schooling, her work path. The only constant had been her grandparents, and it seemed she'd never been emotionally close to them, on top of which she was used to being away from them for long stretches at a time. She'd never had a continuous, tangible presence in her life. Instead, her life, especially in adulthood, had been one long series of fast-paced challenges. It was a rate of change she'd never be able to emulate here.

He was the opposite. For him, routine had always been his saviour. It was the routine and the predictability that allowed him to be the rock that everyone else seemed to rely on—his parents, Chris and to some extent Jules, the hospital, his patients.

He wanted Tilly to stay. But that would tie her down or, worse, it would be like pulling the wings from a butterfly. He wasn't going to be like a little boy, trying to keep captive the very thing he most wanted and killing it in the process. He'd have to leave her free and enjoy the short time they still had before she left and followed her life's work. He wouldn't be responsible for sapping her sparkle and drive, the key to her beauty. She was a free spirit and he loved her that way. He'd have to let her go. And besides, he thought, reading the fax through one more time, did he really have a choice?

Sitting on the front veranda, looking into the bushland surrounding the house as the last rays of the sun touched the sky, was usually a tranquil place for Tilly. But this evening she was restless. She was too keyed up. She'd finally managed to convince Flo she'd be fine out here on her own. She needed solitude as she waited for Jock.

Voices carried to her from inside the house. He was there.

Would he be able to give Flo the hint that they wanted time alone? A few minutes passed before the screen door opened and he emerged, carrying a tray of cold drinks. He was by himself.

'Hi,' she said as he deposited the tray on the table between the two wicker chairs.

'Hi, yourself.' He looked her over. 'You're looking better already.'

'Thanks, but I'm feeling frazzled. I've only been home six hours and Gran is driving me wild.'

'Worrying about you?'

She shuddered. 'By my side from the moment we left the hospital. I'm definitely not used to being fussed over, especially by Gran.'

'Miss Independent.'

'Something like that.' She smiled. 'Except the title is "Doctor", not "Miss".' She was watching him, a little puzzled. She'd been joking about the 'doctor' bit but he seemed not to notice. And there was something in his voice that hadn't been there that afternoon. A reservation? Uncertainty?

'Tilly.'

'Jock.'

They spoke at the same time and awkwardness fell between them until Jock spoke again. 'I brought your mail.' It had been shoved in his pocket and he pulled it out and handed it to her.

'Thanks.' She reached for it and dumped it straight on the side table. 'I'll look at it later. It won't be anything that can't wait.'

'Actually, there is something—' He broke off, and she could see he was embarrassed at having seen something in the pile.

'What is it?' She was laughing. 'I won't shoot the messenger.'

'There's a fax from the aid organisation. It was on the top of the pile.'

'Damn.' She hit her forehead with her palm then picked up the fax and scanned it. 'I'd forgotten about that, with everything that's happened.' She dropped the fax back on the pile. The only thing she was interested in was finishing their conversation from that afternoon. The hours had dragged since he'd gone and she couldn't quite believe he'd started tonight off by focusing on her mail.

'Tilly, about what I said this afternoon, I think you should forget it.'

'What?' Had she heard him right? He was looking stressed and tired, and that wasn't a good sign. 'What do you mean, "forget it"? Forget what? Why?'

'Forget what I said about having time together. I know you're only here for a short while, I've always known that. I just forgot this morning when I realised what you meant to me.'

'But, Jock…'

He sat down next to her and took her hand between his, looking into her eyes as if to convince her he was genuine about what he was saying. 'We're too different, and I'm not going to be the one who tries to stop you from doing what you really want in life just because of how I feel. You're wonderful just the way you are, Tilly, and much as I want to convince you to stay with me, that would amount to me forcing you to change.'

'Jock, what *are* you talking about?' A thought occurred to her. 'Have I had another vague spell? Have I missed something here? I thought you were telling me you cared for me. I thought you wanted to take a chance on us. Now you're saying you don't want to because of who I am? I don't understand.' She felt like pounding her fists on his chest. It made no sense at all.

He shook his head. 'I don't think we can get involved precisely because of how much I love who you are. I don't want you to make sacrifices for me. I don't want you to change.'

'So you don't want to get involved because I'm so great? Jock, I just really, really don't get this. If you've changed your mind about me, tell me. I won't like it, but at least I'll know what on earth is going on.'

'I haven't changed my mind. But you and I are too different, our lives and our worlds are poles apart. Your whole life is filled with different people and places, packed with change and challenges. Life here would never be like that. Life with *me* would never be like that. When I saw that fax, I knew. Even if you think you want to stay, you'd come to regret it. It would only be a short-term reaction to having been ill.' He waved a hand somewhere in the direction of Indonesia. 'That's your world, not this one. Life and work here would very quickly become routine, and I really doubt the words "Tilly" and "routine" have ever been used in the same sentence.'

'Are you telling me even if I feel the same as you and I want to stay, you won't accept that because I'm not thinking straight?'

'I think now is not the time to make life-changing decisions. Not with the week you've just had.'

'Now is exactly the time. Lying in hospital, I was afraid of missing out on my future. My life. And the future I was seeing was here. Not in Indonesia. Or Africa. Or anywhere else I've been. Here. This is where I want to be. And I chose to come back.'

'Because you made a promise to your grandfather, not because you were looking for a new life.'

'That's not right, not entirely. I also needed a break—'

He cut her off. 'Tell me something,' he said, his body language screaming distance at her. 'How long had you been home before you agreed to go back, not just for another three-month contract but to a new posting? A twelve-month one? In Africa?'

She was silent for a moment. He'd take her answer as confirmation of his suspicions. 'I said I'd help them out a couple of days into starting work.'

'So your mind was already turning back there within a week of coming home.'

'It was just a spur-of-the-moment thing. I just asked for more details on a day Gran had been driving me insane. I haven't signed anything. This...' she waved at the fax '...was only confirming the start date *if* I took up the placement. I hadn't made my mind up about my future when I first came back. This was an offer for something new—I had to at least think about it.'

She stopped speaking for a moment, aware her voice was taking on slightly frantic tones and not liking the sound.

'I wasn't sure until I ended up in hospital what I wanted, but there're only so many hours you can mull over the prospect of dying before clarity comes. *Clarity*, Jock, not pie in the sky. Clarity about how I wanted to spend the rest of my life. And although I didn't know if you felt the same, what was clear above all else was that I wanted that life to be here.' She waved a hand at the bush, in the opposite direction to which he'd waved moments before. 'Not in Africa. Or Indonesia. And more to the point…' she took a deep breath '…with you.' His expression remained impassive. 'Is there nothing I can say to convince you I mean that?'

'You don't belong here. You'd come to see that in time.'

It hit her then. She'd realised Jock Kelly's side was where she belonged but he didn't agree. He was trying to extract himself from her. *He* was the one who'd acted too quickly on today. He'd confused stress and emotion over his property and his brother with his feelings for her. Now he'd realised and he didn't know how to tell her he had to break free.

'I think I understand. You took responsibility for me, too, while I was sick, just like your family. You think I'll be another chain just when you've freed yourself of your brother.'

'You think I'm trying to tell you I'm unburdening myself of you?'

She nodded. That was exactly what she thought.

'Trust me, Tilly, you're no burden. It's exactly the opposite.'

'What, then?'

'If you stay, *I'd* be the burden. I can't leave my work—I have the unit to finish for a start. My life and my work are here, yours aren't.'

'I can decide that for myself, Jock. Let me put it this way. You can refuse to get involved with me, that's your choice. But you can't refuse to let me stay in Noosa. That's my choice. And I'd really, really like it if you'd be happy about that and take a chance on me. And stop telling me I'm not thinking straight when I *know* I've never had a better thought in my life.'

She could see the first sign of him wavering.

There was only one thing to do.

She slid out of her chair and onto his lap before he could stop her, and took his face between her hands. 'I'm going to kiss you now, Jock Kelly, and, dammit, when I've finished you'll see what I'm trying to tell you.'

She lowered her mouth to touch the corner of his lips. Her touch was light. She had every intention of teasing him, drawing out the moment until she kissed him properly, giving him time to realise he couldn't end things between them.

She pressed her lips against the other side of his mouth and traced her fingers gently over the slight roughness of his skin.

But then he parted his lips ever so slightly and she didn't know who gave in first, but they were kissing with an intensity that pulled her into a world that didn't exist beyond the two of them. He was holding her face between his hands now and she'd slid hers around to rest on his back, to pull him towards her until they were as close as possible.

The warmth of his lips contrasted to the coolness of his teeth, the smoothness of the skin on his back where she'd slipped her hands under his top was at odds with the texture of the skin on his face, which was grazing slightly against her own. Her senses were going into overdrive, the scent of him rich and warm and wonderful. There was nothing but Jock, she thought as she sank deeper into the most wonderful kiss imaginable.

A kiss wasn't enough.

She was in his blood and it wasn't just a matter of wanting her, it was a matter of life not being able to continue until they'd savoured every tiny part of each other and then started all over again.

She pulled away, just a little, and he heard himself groan as the intensity of the contact ended.

He opened his eyes and looked straight into hers, still so close that he could see the tiny flecks of gold in her irises, the thin circle that wasn't drowned out by the largeness of her inky black pupils. He should say something but his head was swimming and he was unable to form words.

'You still think…' Her voice was a husky whisper as she traced a single finger down the hard bones of his spine. 'I don't know what I want?'

He shook his head to clear a path for speech when his mind was half on the feeling of her fingernail scraping so lightly against his skin. 'I don't know, Tilly.' He had to stop and clear his throat. 'But I'm hoping you do. That was some kiss.'

'I thought it might knock some sense into you.'

'You thought right.'

'Good.' She bent her head down so her nose was resting against his. 'Because nothing has ever made this much sense. Ever.'

'I've run out of arguments. I can't resist you.' He touched her bottom lip with his thumb. 'So I'll only ask once more. Do you think you can be happy here?'

'I could be happy anywhere, as long as it's with you.'

'And your aid work?'

'Maybe one day I'll convince you to come with me for a few months, just so you can see it for yourself. But if that never happens, that would be just fine by me. I've done what I wanted to do. I've made my contribution and I know I'm entitled to start a life for me now. I've proved all I needed to prove. You say it will be routine here and you wonder if I'll get bored. You know what I think?'

'What?'

'I think routine sounds like the most wonderful word in the

world. It doesn't have to mean humdrum, Jock. Life with you could never be that. But stability, knowing where we're headed, knowing we're doing it together, sounds like heaven to me.' She dropped another kiss square on his lips and he went to hold her to him, but she slipped away again. 'You call it routine. I call it having a home with a heart. I call it belonging.'

'So you know what you're doing?'

'I know I've fancied the pants off you from the first moment we met and it's taken almost no time to see I was quite right to feel that way.'

'There's that forward Tilly I've grown to know and love so well.'

'Love?'

'Haven't I said that yet?'

She shook her head, a big, beautiful smile on her face.

'I love you.' He kissed her and this time she went to continue the kiss and he was the one to pull back. 'I love you with every ounce of who I am and I love every ounce of who you are.'

'And you...' she twisted on his lap so she could tuck her head in under his chin '...are the best welcome-home present a woman could ever have. It was very clever of you to employ me.'

'I'll take credit for it, sure.'

'Actually, now that I think of it, we would've met anyway.' Her smile was light and teasing, full of happiness. 'Neighbour.'

'Let's just agree,' he said, as he caressed the fullness of her mouth with his gaze, 'that it was meant to be.'

She could see he was going to make her wait to be kissed again and waiting wasn't her strong point. 'Seal it with a kiss?'

'Since you've even brushed your hair for me...' he'd taken hold of a length of it now, loose over her shoulders, and was running it thoughtfully between his fingers '...there's no way I can refuse.'

'Don't tease. I've just come out of hospital.'

'You're stronger than that, Jungle Tilly.' And with one swift movement he scooped her up in his arms and turned her so her mouth was beneath his own. She had just a second to catch her breath with surprise before he brought his mouth down to cover hers in a kiss so intense she was immediately lost in the sensation of his lips over hers.

And ten minutes or twenty or one hour later, as they drew apart, all she could think to murmur was, 'If you're going to kiss me like that when I do my hair, I can't wait to see what's on offer when I paint my toenails.'

'Tilly, we've only just begun and I think we've got quite some journey ahead of us.'

EPILOGUE

'GLAD to be home?' Jock deposited their hand luggage at his wife's feet as they stood at the carousel, waiting for their bags.

'Home.' Tilly smiled up at him. 'Yes, I am. I'm even looking forward to seeing Gran and your siblings.'

'Even Chris?'

'Yep. From what Jules has said, he seems happy being an employee again and seems to be making a good living.'

'All thanks to you. I should have met you years ago—you could have straightened out my whole family.'

'I am your family now.'

'Soon to be a family of three.' Jock pulled his wife into his side and touched the swell of her stomach he was convinced he could detect. 'Hi, there, baby, how'd you enjoy your first flight?'

Tilly grinned and pressed her hand over his. She still couldn't believe she was married to this wonderful man.

'And you're sure you're ready to settle down in one spot?' he asked.

'Positive. I've definitely ticked the overseas aid work box on my list of things to do. Whereas you...'

'Whereas I, as much as I enjoyed my brief foray into your previous life, am also pleased to be back. Especially under such happy circumstances. So let's get our things and go home.'

'There's one of ours,' she said as her battered, dusty backpack swung around on the conveyer belt. Jock was elbowed out of the way by another traveller and missed the pack.

If she stood on tiptoe, maybe she could watch her bag go round again and make sure no one else grabbed it by mistake before Jock could get it. Not that anyone would want her luggage. It was in far worse shape than any of the other bags circling on the belt—mostly they were smart suitcases on wheels. The sound of a baby gurgling distracted her and she watched as the child's mother bounced the baby gently in her arms. She was also yet to fully convince herself that in six months or so she and Jock would be parents. And tease her as he might about her conviction, she knew their baby would be a little boy with grey eyes who looked just like his father. And she would be like that mother over there, showering her baby with kisses.

'There's still six months to go, wife of mine, so quit staring at babies and let's get home.' Jock was back at her side, luggage at his feet.

'Where's my pack?' she asked as she looked down at the mound of gear beside them.

'Here.' Jock touched the pack closest to her with his foot.

'That's not mine.' She looked back at the carousel and pointed. 'That's mine.'

Jock, grumbling good-naturedly and tossing the pack back on the carousel, grabbing hers a moment later.

'They looked the same to me.' He laughed as he returned to her side. 'Not a clean patch on either of them.'

'Don't laugh, it's insulting.' But she was laughing, too. 'Those packs are well travelled. '

'And you wonder why you always get held up by Customs. I think it might have something to do with this.' He touched her old trekking sandals with the tip of his still new-looking boot. 'And this,' he said as he flicked the cuff of her khaki pants with his knee just below the zip line where they could be unattached to form long shorts. 'And this,' he added as he pointed to her worn backpack.

'That's judgmental,' she sniffed.

'Judgmental or not, I like you this way. I hardly recognised you on our honeymoon when you wore new shoes.'

'So you'll still love me when I'm wearing the same tracksuit four days in a row and covered in baby's mess?'

'Even more.'

'Really?'

'Maybe not four days.' He rubbed at his chin while he mulled over the prospect of parenthood. 'Can we compromise on three? And the odd shower?'

'I can manage that. And, Jock?'

'Yes?'

'Just for the record, we've been back in Australia…' she glanced at her watch '…for almost forty minutes and you haven't kissed me.'

'How very remiss of me. Would you have time for me to remedy that now?'

Her answer was stifled as he bent his head and took her mouth in a kiss that she could think of only one word to describe.

Home.

She was home.

With Jock. And soon they'd have their baby. And if 'routine' could possibly cover as wonderful a prospect as that, then routine was the most beautiful thing that had ever happened to her.

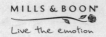

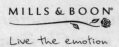

Latin Affairs

Featuring
The Sicilian's Passion by Sharon Kendrick
In the Spaniard's Bed by Helen Bianchin
The Italian Marriage by Kathryn Ross

Make sure you buy these irresistible stories!

On sale 1st December 2006

*Available at WHSmith, Tesco, ASDA, Borders, Eason,
Sainsbury's and most bookshops*

www.millsandboon.co.uk

FREE

4 BOOKS AND A SURPRISE GIFT!

We would like to take this opportunity to thank you for reading this Mills & Boon® book by offering you the chance to take FOUR more specially selected titles from the Medical Romance™ series absolutely FREE! We're also making this offer to introduce you to the benefits of the Mills & Boon® Reader Service™—

★ **FREE home delivery**
★ **FREE gifts and competitions**
★ **FREE monthly Newsletter**
★ **Books available before they're in the shops**
★ **Exclusive Reader Service offers**

Accepting these FREE books and gift places you under no obligation to buy; you may cancel at any time, even after receiving your free shipment. Simply complete your details below and return the entire page to the address below. You don't even need a stamp!

YES! Please send me 4 free Medical Romance books and a surprise gift. I understand that unless you hear from me, I will receive 6 superb new titles every month for just £2.80 each, postage and packing free. I am under no obligation to purchase any books and may cancel my subscription at any time. The free books and gift will be mine to keep in any case.

M6ZEE

Ms/Mrs/Miss/Mr...Initials ....
BLOCK CAPITALS PLEASE

Surname ....

Address ....

....

....Postcode ....

Send this whole page to:
The Reader Service, FREEPOST CN81, Croydon, CR9 3WZ